5/30/99

To Monica —
 Sorry you couldn't make it to Memphis, but your husband was thinking of you —
 Best regards,
 William Watkins

Cassina Gambrel Was Missing

WILLIAM WATKINS

CASSINA GAMBREL WAS MISSING

A NOVEL

LYNX PUBLISHING COMPANY
NEW YORK

CASSINA GAMBREL WAS MISSING.
Copyright © 1999 by William B. Watkins. All rights reserved. Printed in the United States of America. No part of this book may be used or reproduced in any manner whatsoever without written permission except in the case of brief quotations embodied in critical articles or reviews. For information, address:
Lynx Publishing Company, P.O. Box 30275, New York, NY 10011.

ISBN 0-9668965-0-5

Library of Congress Catalog Card Number: 98-96863

First published in the United States of America by Lynx Publishing Company.

First Lynx Publishing Company Edition: April 1999

10 9 8 7 6 5 4 3 2 1

"The Aba Daba Honeymoon" words and music by
Arthur Fields and Walter Donovan.

Lyric excerpts of "Getting to Know You" by Richard Rodgers
and Oscar Hammerstein II appear on pages 57-59.
Copyright © 1951 by Richard Rodgers and Oscar Hammerstein II
Copyright Renewed. WILLIAMSON MUSIC owner of publication
and allied rights throughout the world.
International Copyright Secured   Reprinted by Permission
All Rights Reserved.

"Lift Every Voice and Sing"
James Weldon Johnson and J. Rosamond Johnson.
Used by permission of EDWARD B. MARKS MUSIC COMPANY.

A portion of the poem "Winter Remembered" by John Crowe Ransom,
copyright 1924 by Alfred A. Knopf, Inc. and renewed 1952
by John Crowe Ransom is reprinted from
Selected Poems, Third Edition, Revised and Enlarged
by John Crowe Ransom by permission of Alfred A. Knopf, Inc.

For my parents
and the students of Southwestern at Memphis

Chapter One

Shvarzers

"LORD," SAID CASSINA Gambrel, settling her hindquarters on a bench by the fountain in Court Square, "just look at all the *shvarzers*. There sure are a lot of *shvarzers* downtown today!"

I choked on my Coca-Cola, sending it dribbling down my chin. I couldn't have heard that. She couldn't have said it. "What on earth … what are you saying?" Then, giving her the benefit of the doubt—"Cassina, do you know what a *shvarzer* is?" I sucked a straw full of cola to try to clear my throat. Dumb.

"Well, I reckon they's cars. Miss Esther always says, 'You cain't go anyplace downtown anymore for all the *shvarzers*!'"

When the Coke stopped running out of my nostrils, I set it down. Somehow, I'd lost my taste for it.

Now, I know you'll think it unusual that Cassina Gambrel and I ever became friends, ridiculous that we would even be sitting on the same bench. I should tell you now that this will not be the story you want to hear, told as you want to hear it. You will probably only focus on the obvious differences between us: Not the least of which is the difference in our ages. Truth is, I didn't really know how old Cassina was at the time. In those days, I never thought much about the subject of age. Not like today, at thirty-eight, when I grow more conscious of it every day. Then, people over, say, thirty-five or so were simply lumped together in an undefinable group until they were "old" (sixty?). At a family gathering about three years ago, I discovered this still to be a widespread phenomenon among younger people when a distant cousin, a lovely seventeen year old, called me "sir". They tell me she's healing.

That encounter may be the thing that has set my mind in overdrive these last few years thinking on my own youth (a word I hate for all its connotations) and the friends I had. I want to tell you this story—the story of how Cassina Gambrel and I became friends—because Cassina truly was a friend, someone you should know, whatever her exact position on the scale between "young" and "old".

A great advantage to being as young as I was then was—is—that it never entered my mind that there should be any sort of barrier between us. At that age, the world was still "brave" and "new" in a lot of ways: Independence (so I thought) from Mom and Dad back in Knoxville; living with a roommate off-campus in a big, wicked city.

It was July 1978—the summer I did the internship at that bank in downtown Memphis following my sophomore year at Southwestern. Part of my job was to ferry Cassina back and forth as necessary from the East Memphis home of Mr. Edward Meyerman, the founder and chairman of the bank, for whose wife she worked. Cassina would deliver mail or other papers from the house to Mr. Meyerman's office when he was in town, perform any necessary errands downtown or at any point along our ten mile route west on Poplar to Union Avenue, then on to the bank tower rising above Court Square. We would pick up everything from opera tickets to dry cleaning on our circuit and the whole thing was charged to the company.

I am certain Cassina, herself, was on the bank's payroll, not Mrs. Meyerman's. How they justified that is not exactly known to me. I was a twenty year old intern and knew enough not to ask too many questions (at least not in certain circles). There was still enough good-old-boy clout in Memphis in those days to get away with a lot if you were of a certain level—and Meyerman certainly was. Understand that it was not so long ago, really, just long enough for the world to be a little bit different. Better? Worse? You decide. Different.

Our routine, marked by polite Good mornings and Isn't the weather awfuls, lasted six weeks before Cassina and I decided on this fourteenth day of July, that we would vary the pattern and have an *al fresco* lunch before taking her back "Out East" as it's called. Both of us must have sensed that, by now, it was time to let down our hair a little. First purchasing two hot dogs apiece, a large Dr. Pepper in a cup for her, and a Coca-Cola for me from a little stand on the Mall, we made our way over to Court Square, me mopping sweat from my face the whole time.

If you have ever been to Memphis in the summertime, there is no need for me to tell you that the word "hot" does not quite describe it. You know how people in Arizona always say clever things like, "It's a dry heat, so you don't notice it"? Well, in Memphis, it's a *wet* heat; therefore, downright God-awful some days.

Especially downtown, close to the Mississippi. Which is where we were. Foolishly.

Maybe, though, if we had been inside in the air conditioning among the sane people, we might not have been talking as freely as we were. Or rather, she was. I am sure that in a crowded café, she would never have dared to tell me the story that, without warning, I found myself caught up in that day as I sat in the Victorian splendor of Court Square drenched with soda. Almost sure.

"No, sir," Cassina went on, "Miss Esther is right about that. You sure cain't." Giving my predicament with the soft-drink scant attention, she said, "You be careful now, I had a cousin to *drown* on one of those things once," before confiding, "I figured at first that *shvarzers* was pigeons. That was the only thing I could think of that there was more of down here than out where she stays—Miss Esther, I mean. Then I figured not."

There was more.

"One day, I was down here in this very square after doing some shopping over to Lowenstein's department store and the pigeons was everywhere. Now you know I cain't stand those things—rats with wings 'swhat I say. And I was sittin' ... " she pointed to a bench just beyond the fountain " ... right over there, eatin' a little slice of pound cake I had brought with me for a snack in case I got hungry (you know, shoppin' always does just zap my strength), and the pigeons was everywhere, just *every*where! Flyin' down and peckin' at the crumbs at my feet, wobblin' around in that dumb-ass way of their's and making that stupid warbling noise they make—you know the one I mean—that 'coo, coo, brr, brr' sound." She made the noise in the back of her mouth, letting it slide down her throat to her chest for the latter part, punctuating each pair of sounds with double thrusts of her chin.

My eyebrows flew up as I stared open-mouthed at her, then plummeted in a furrow, eyes narrowing into two scrutinizing slits—*Is she toying with me?* My head cocked automatically to one side as I surveyed her.

"That's it!" she cried out, waving her index finger, chubby as a parsnip, in my face. "You look just like one! That stupid thing they do with their heads. I tell you, I do know for sure where they get that expression 'bird-brain' from." Giving me a sideways glance—"Let's just say they ain't exactly the smartest creatures the Almighty ever breathed life into!" She shifted her weight and tugged absent-mindedly at one bra strap through her starched, white blouse. "Hot, itn't it?"

I managed some vaguely affirmative gesture.

"Anyways, so there I was, eating my cake, and these damn birds were gathering 'round me, and another one swooping down out of the sky like something in a Alfred Hitchcock picture or something. Finally, I couldn't stand it no more and jumped up, waving my arms, stamping my feet, and saying, 'Shoo! Shoo! Get on outta' here. Go on, you stupid *shvarzers*, get away!' " A big hearty laugh came thundering out of her with such force that her ample bosoms shook in response.

Throughout her entire story, I found my hand repeatedly returning to cover my mouth.

Cassina wiped a tear from her eye with the back of her hand and slapped her neck. "Well, I must've looked quite a sight 'cause I looked over to see Mr. Abraham Waxman of *the* Waxmans who own all that property down here along the river, *that* one, you know. He was sittin' right here on this very bench where we's sittin' and he was starin' down at me like I'd gone stark ravin' mad."

I could only imagine why.

"Pretty soon, Mr. Waxman come over and said to me, 'Hello, Cassina', and I said, 'How-do, Mr. Waxman.' (Mr. Waxman and I have known each other for years on account of I cooked at the Yeshiva where his two boys went and then at his synagogue many times when there was some special affair or other.) And Mr. Waxman, who was always a real gentleman, said to me, 'Cassina, how are you feeling today?' and I say, 'Oh, fine, Mr. Waxman, just fine, thank you. I do reckon I look a sight jumpin' up and down in the Court Square 'n' all. But I tell you true, it's just all these *shvarzers* everywhere. I cain't stand 'em. You cain't go anywhere downtown without 'em being everywhere.'

"And he looked at me kinda' funny-like and said, 'Cassina, those are not *shvarzers*.' I said, 'No, Mr. Waxman?' and he shook his head and said in that gentle way of his, 'No, Cassina. I do believe somebody's told you wrong.'

" 'Oh my!' I said then, feeling kinda' embarrassed in case I had said somethin' just awful. 'You know, Mr. Waxman, I always was afraid of sayin' anything in a foreign tongue case I got it wrong and said somethin' downright obscene. Hinkey-Dinkey-Parlez-Vous—you know what I mean?' "

She sang the last line to me with a laugh to demonstrate.

"Well, Mr. Waxman and I, we had ourselves a right good laugh about that, and I finally says to him, 'But Mr. Waxman, if it ain't too awful, would you mind tellin' me what a *shvarzer* is?' Then I tol' him what Miss Esther said (you know, what I tol' you about not bein' able to go downtown anymore 'n' all) and he looked at me kinda' sad, almost like he was gonna' cry right there on the spot. I know'd he was kinda' what you'd call an 'emotional' fellow, so I says to him, 'Now, Mr. Waxman, it's all right. You don't havta' tell me if you don't wanta.'

"He took out his hankie to blow his nose and when he did, his sleeve dropped back off his bare wrist a few inches and I could see that place where he had been tattooed with a number from his days before he came to this country." Her voice grew soft as she spoke. "And I reached out my hand, patted him on the shoulder and said, 'There, there. It's all right, Mr. Waxman.' He looked at me again, quiet-like, and said, 'Come along.' "

Cassina paused. She took a bite of her hot dog, then daubed at the corners of her mouth with her paper napkin before smoothing it out on her lap with three luxuriant strokes as if it were fine linen. Maybe this is when she drew breath. God knows the woman could talk.

"So we walked over there to the edge of the square,"—she motioned in the general direction—"and he said, 'Let's just wait a minute, Cassina.' So we waited. Before long, wouldn't you know it, my neighbor Emma's son, Russell, comes drivin' along in his big black Lincoln. Black as the ace of spades—the car, I mean. Well, I wave hello and Russell waves back. Mr. Waxman, he waves and Russell waves at him and we're all standin' there on the street wavin' 'hey!' like country-come-home.

"Well, Russell drives off and Mr. Waxman smiles his sorta' sad smile again. He just waits patiently like we got all the time in the world.

"In another minute, another fellow drives by in his big black Pontiac and we all wave how-do. Mr. Waxman don't say nothin'. Traffic backs up there 'round 2nd Street for some reason or other and this bein' downtown and all, some fool starts honkin' his horn. Then somebody else does. And then there's some words spoken and a regular little commotion brewin' over nothin' at all. Mr. Waxman looks at me with his lips drawn-in in a tight little line, gives a sigh through his nose, and nods in an understanding way like he's sayin', 'Yes, yes ... oh, Lordy, yes.'

"I give it right back to him—noddin' and sighing and throwing in a little 'tut-tut-tut' to boot."

Cassina and I were both nodding.

"Finally, he says to me, 'So, Cassina, now you know.'

" '*Nu*, already, Mr. Waxman,' I says to him, 'what can you do?'

"He nods 'yes' some more. We both nod 'til our heads are about to fall off.

" 'Mr. Waxman,' I say, 'I sure do appreciate knowin' you. Just wait 'til I tell Miss Esther I found out what a *shvarzer* is.'

"Well, Mr. Waxman, he laughed right out loud. Threw his head back, dropped his chin, and let out with a big old 'Har! Har!' liked I never heard before."

Hearing her tell it, I laughed, too. "Well, Cassina," I finally asked, "Did you tell her?"

"In my fashion," she responded. "You know," she said, shaking an admonishing finger at my food, "you haven't eaten a bite. It's a sin to waste food."

I had been too enraptured to notice, so while she waited, I took a big bite of hot dog and began to chew.

Cassina gave an approving nod and wink before explaining. "I jus' began using that word in my regular conversation with her."

"What do you mean?" I said through a mouth full of food.

"Well, for example, whenever I go someplace that I know Miss Esther just loves to go, I give her a little report. 'Miss Esther,' I says, 'This town sure is growin'.'

" 'Yes, it is, Cassina,' she'll say.

" 'Why, you cain't go anywhere nowadays for all the *shvarzers*. I was on the expressway goin' downtown and the *shvarzers* was everywhere!' Or 'You shoulda' seen the *shvarzers* around Overton Park today, Miss Esther. You couldn't get through there for all the *shvarzers*! By the way, Miss Esther, I hear they are even tryin' to get the Interstate to go right through the park nowadays. Tore down a whole bunch of those fine old houses in Midtown just to make it easier for the *shvarzers*. Imagine, all those *shvarzers* plowing right through that beautiful park, smack through the middle of the zoo and right on into downtown. Thousands of 'em everyday. Then thousands more coming this direction— all the way from California! Picture it, Miss Esther: *Shvarzers* coming all across the West, across Oklahoma—sweepin' down the plain, into Arkansas, and right on to Memphis, straight through the park and out this way. Day and night. Lord! Just think of the noise, Miss Esther. And the smell.' "

I choked again.

There was no stopping her. " 'An' Miss Esther, I declare, even way out in the rich suburbs, way out to Germantown (now I know you love it out there, Miss Esther), the number of *shvarzers* you see is amazing. It used to be so peaceful, too! Why, even yesterday at the opening of the Germantown Charity Horse Show, there was a line of *shvarzers* just waitin' to get in—big ones, too—backed up all the way down the highway into East Memphis. They had out a special patrol to handle 'em all. You be careful when you go out there now, Miss Esther, you hear?' "

Cassina kept a poker face the whole time she told me this, which only had me laughing so hard I almost peed my pants. "Now, Cassina ... "

"But do you know, Miss Esther just looked kinda' pale? White as a sheet—if you'll pardon the expression." Cassina leaned in towards me as if the next thing were a secret. "She didn't go to the Horse Show this year. Come to think of it," she added, "Miss Esther don't go too many places nowadays. Just stays shut up ... shut up like a prisoner in her own little world."

"You're terrible," I said.

She put her right hand up in the air, testifying. "It's true, I know. Somebody like me talking about a lady like her. I know."

I looked at Cassina and she looked at me, blinking only once. Then her mighty brown eyes narrowed slightly and she smiled a smile so enigmatic that the Mona Lisa, herself, would have blushed at the competition.

So, already—to coin Cassina's phrase—now you know. Maybe now that I'm all grown up, now that I know so much, I would do different. But I was young then, sittin' on that bench. And you tell me: What else could I have done ... but to love her? It was the Christian thing to do.

Chapter Two

***"I'd Rather Be Here
Than Any Place I Know"
—W.C. Handy***

LOVE HER? OF course, I did, although at first I did not recognize it as such. "Awe" is a more precise term for what I felt when I looked at Cassina Gambrel. There she stood like some great monument, distinctly different from me in most every way, reminding me that she was everything I was not: Outrageously funny, clever, a daredevil, and apparently, it seemed, very confident in her every move. I wasn't. Not that I was an oaf, merely inexperienced and not much of a talker. In that respect, we were most definitely a fine match. For the remainder of the summer, Cassina talked and I listened, usually with mouth agape.

Though not articulate, I did have a brain, a good one at that. I had scored over 1500 on the SATs my senior year in high school and had something of a knack for writing, but chiefly, I was good with figures. Math came easily for some reason and while most of my high school comrades were stumbling and tripping over basic trigonometry's tan, sine, and cosine, I was racing along like an Olympian, taking, what were to me, those small hurdles and more advanced ones easily.

To the delight of my parents, I had scored high enough on an Advanced Placement test as a senior to allow me to earn college credit while still in high school, thereby skipping the first two terms of college math altogether.

Good scores also earned me a generous scholarship to Southwestern, a fine liberal arts college in Memphis (the school has since changed its name). Money in our family was tight, but with further aid from the Knoxville Rotary Club, I matriculated in the Fall Term, 1976, planning a course of study in Business Math.

Come to think of it, from this juncture, I can not imagine mapping out a more boring existence for myself. It was a safe road, though, the one I planned to take, through times that were still somewhat turbulent. Yes, things had calmed down considerably by then from the great upheaval of the 1960's and early '70's, but the dust was still settling and exactly what had been wrought was not yet entirely clear. President Nixon, who had appeared to be the great hope for the vast majority of conservative Americans—and my family wanted to count themselves well within that number when any saints did any marching in—had resigned only two short years before. To folks like us in Knoxville who thought of ourselves not at all as backward, but rather "decent," that had proved to be a sore blow, a dashing of dreams. I know that a lot of other people felt that way, too, but I often wonder if for so many people in America, far removed from the power centers in Washington, New York, and the major cities, that signaled their complete loss of control over what their lives and worlds were all about. Maybe understanding something about all that will help you to understand also why I ended up on the road that I did.

Despite all the upheaval (or maybe because of it), everyone was eager to get on with things, I do know that. The administration of Gerald Ford had been a band-aid and the election of Jimmy Carter eight weeks after I began college was to some, a sign of re-birth, putting the past behind and moving ahead with what we hoped was the promise.

I stood ready, too, to the best of my eighteen-year-old abilities, feeling somewhat noble and a whole lot wide-eyed. Studying in Memphis, where, only a few years before, Martin Luther King had been assassinated and National Guard tanks rolled down the streets, seemed like being in another world. Knoxville was home to the University of Tennessee, which I could easily have attended, but Memphis was a sprawling river city, a mass of contradictions, which, while still within the boundaries of the same state, was in an altogether different place, holding great appeal to me as a symbol of something new (while still being somewhat "safe").

Like Cassina, I was, or rather am, it would be more proper to say in my case, a Tennessee native, but the differences between the worlds of Knoxville, situated in the Appalachian Mountains in the eastern part of the state, and Memphis, three-hundred-fifty miles west, are vast. They have essentially different histories and politics as well as very different accents. Mine may not be beautiful to some and I have taken my share of ribbing about it, notably when I first moved to Massachusetts, right after college, but Cassina's accent was downright hysterical to me with its odd mix of Delta smoothness, midwestern flatness, and dash of Tennessee twang topping it off. That, and her liberal co-opting of words and phrases from other languages to suit her needs.

Cassina's name was also peculiar to me, and were I truly the Southern gentleman that so many fought so hard to make me, I would not mention it, since, of course, she had nothing to do with it and therefore—in the Southern scheme of things—changing it would simply have been gauche. It was a fitting name it turned out—what with its spicy redolence of vice—for I am always reminded of gambling when I hear it. As I had discovered that day in Court Square, being with Cassina Gambrel was a chancy thing, sort of like dropping a quarter in a slot machine and pulling a lever. That day, I had got lucky.

As for me, I was named, not, as you may think, for the seventh president of these Newnited States (and one of the founders of Memphis, coincidentally)—well, that was not the *primary* reason for my name, at least. Rather, much more simply, my mother's maiden name was Jackson. Andrew was actually the Christian name of my paternal great-grandfather, a Virginia farmer who died long before I was born. It is also a name my mother happened to like, being the name of one of her favorite saints: Andrew was the disciple who introduced his more famous brother, Peter, to Jesus. In the Gospel According to John, Andrew literally "brought Peter to Jesus." Naming me this satisfied something deep within Mother's formidable evangelical background. Dad was an Episcopalian—'nough said.

I was not called "Andrew Taylor" (and thank God, because I never would have survived my childhood, growing up in the shadow of "The Andy Griffith Show") simply because Dad thought "A. Jackson Taylor" more distinguished and also because the habit of naming (especially) a first child with the last names of both parents is one of the South's more particularly peculiar institutions, as if everyone needed to be reminded that the product was a collaborative effort.

It could have been worse. Heaven only knows how many Brown Butts there are running around the vast environs of Dixie, or how many Ramsey Balls have suffered the slings and arrows of their own outrageous misfortune. It gives one pause. My old roommate, Braden O'Brien, once swore to me that he had gone to high school with a Cooke Weldon. Believe me, there are days when I have sunk to my knees and thanked the Almighty that I got off so easily.

The female equivalent of this curse, to my way of thinking, is the cute double name. (I have to admit finding the maiden name–surname thing in women somehow attractive.) The double name bit has been parodied *ad infinitum*, I know, to the pain of Peggy Sues, Bitsy Maries, and Loula Maes everywhere. And while I am aware it is not *entirely* true that Southern girls are expected to be double-monickered (or, at the very least, hyphenated), I believe the following speaks for itself:

There was a shy and rather pretty girl of my acquaintance back in Knoxville by the simple name of Susan Bell—"Suzy" to all who knew her. At a social event, she found herself, unexpectedly, in the company of a lady of a certain age to whom she had not been introduced. After chatting for a few minutes, the lady, being quite gracious, extended her hand to our Suzy to introduce herself (there being no one else conveniently situated at the moment to accomplish the formalities). "I'm Mrs. Glockenspiel," she announced.

"How do you do?" came the quiet and perfectly polite, though inadequate, response.

The older lady—being a lady—sensed the awkwardness of her younger companion and gently prodded, "And what is your name, dear?"

"Suzy Bell."

Mrs. Glockenspiel smiled sweetly; this was going to be harder than she thought: "Suzy-Bell what?"

I HAD BEEN in search of something new and Cassina Gambrel was about as new as I could get. I'd never seen anything like her. I was somewhat shy ... is that the right word? ... quiet?—better. Managed to hold my own at school, but Cassina was not like anyone at school—not the women my age, not even like the most boisterous faculty members.

The internship at the bank, which had been arranged through the head of my department (Meyerman also served on the Board of Directors at Southwestern) afforded me a good opportunity to get my feet wet in the business world and earn academic credit. It was routine stuff that I did mostly—I was a glorified office-boy who had a list of goals to accomplish including interfacing with staff throughout the bank and, ostensibly to learn from them, interviewing executives about their experience. A paper summarizing my own experiences would follow, as would performance evaluations from my supervisor. My jaunts with Cassina became a nice break and following that memorable day in Court Square, is it any wonder I looked forward to them?

Now the traffic situation in Memphis is unbelievably bad. About that time (1978), one of the major television networks actually broadcast a piece about the insurance industry voting Memphis drivers the worst in the world. I am afraid that's a true thing and Cassina and I did our level best to keep the title. One afternoon, on the late end of the lunch rush, Cassina had to make a stop for Mrs. Meyerman to return something to a store located in a strip shopping center in East Memphis.

"Whoa, stop!" she cried out.

"What?" I thought there was some sort of emergency. "What happened?"

"Stop! Turn here."

"Where?"

"Here, here!" She pointed frantically to a spot on my side of the car.

"Here?" A combination clock and thermometer like one of those outside of some banks stood sentinel by the entranceway to the shopping plaza. "I have to turn left across three lanes of traffic!"

"This is it!" she screamed as if the world were coming to an end.

It almost did. I hit the brakes, hoping we would not be rammed from behind. Tires squealed, horns sounded, deities were invoked.

"Why didn't you tell me a mile ago?" I yelled at her. "Jesus, Cassina!"

She shot an admonishing look at me. "Watch your mouth!" Then, added simply, "I forgot."

A glance in the rearview mirror showed a long line of cars halted behind me. Flicking the turn signal with my little finger, I inched slowly over into the turning lane running down the center of the street and managed to pull the company's Oldsmobile 88 behind a Buick and a VW Bug waiting there. Looking back, and trying hard not to catch the eye of the driver immediately behind us, I could see traffic beginning to edge slowly around the rear of our car.

My hands covered my face and slowly slid down until my fingertips tugged at the skin beneath my lower eyelids exposing the red area—a pig face almost or like that Munsch painting, you know, *The Scream*. Without turning my head, I rolled my eyes sideways towards her and stared silently.

"Well ... " was all she said. It came out in a semi-exasperated, semi-whine that arched across two syllables: "Way-uhl."

A full ten minutes later, we were able to make the turn, thanks only to the mercy shown us by drivers in the opposing lanes who were stopped by a traffic light. Once across, we sat again in a line of cars waiting for a parking space.

I looked at her again.

"Well ... " she said once more, a bit more firmly. She clutched at the red shopping bag sitting in her lap.

"What's in there, anyway?"

"A blender," she muttered.

"A what?"

"A blender," she repeated loudly, shifting and pulling herself upright.

"A blender," I repeated.

"A blender," she said with relish, squeezing the bag to her chest as if it were a gift for the Christ child.

"Oh, a *blender*," I replied. "Had I only known. I thought perhaps it was something unimportant." (Cassina was rubbing off on me already.)

"Miss Esther needs her blender fixed."

"Somebody sure needs something fixed!" I peeked in the mirror again at the traffic behind us. The *shvarzers* were everywhere.

"All right," Cassina protested. "We didn't get killed or nothing!"

"Merely by the grace of You-Know-Who!"

Just then, there came a rapping sound at the window. I looked quickly. Two knuckles came towards me, striking at the glass again. Behind them, a woman's face, about thirty, pinched into a tight grimace, looking not at all unlike the grillwork of an Edsel.

I cranked the window down. The woman's face loomed through.

"Do you know you've been holding up traffic for half an hour?" she screamed.

"Me? I ... "

"You've kept everybody waiting!"

"What?" I looked around. Cassina and I were in one of many cars lined up in the parking lot.

"Nobody can get through because of you two!" She glared at Cassina.

I was stunned. The woman was raving. Maybe it was the heat. I began rolling up the window.

"How dare you!" the woman screamed. She looked again at Cassina, then at me. "I ought to have the two of you arrested!"

"That's it!" cried Cassina. Her hand was on the door handle and she was shoving the hallowed blender to me at the same time. She was out the door before I knew what was happening.

I watched from within, like being at a drive-in movie, as Cassina barreled around the front of the car, pushing imaginary sleeves up over her elbows.

"All right, let's go!" she yelled at the woman who backed two steps away from the car. "You lookin' for a fight? Let's fight!"

The woman's jaw worked, but no sound came out.

Cassina took another step forward to the two steps back of the woman. I hunkered down to see out, bobbing and weaving my head like a boxer.

"You sure are quiet now," Cassina said to her. "Somethin' wrong?"

"I ... I ... " stammered the terrified woman.

"You got quite a nerve, don'cha?" she snapped. "All of us here, waitin' our turn. Actin' like ladies and gentlemen. Makin' out the best we can in a bad situation and in this terrible heat, too!" I looked, and indeed sweat was pouring off of Cassina. The digital clock/thermometer by the driveway read ninety-eight degrees.

The other woman was ashen, her mouth twitching frantically.

"An' you wantin' to blow off some steam on the rest of us. Pickin' on that poor, innocent boy!"

Oh, God! I slid down in the seat.

Cassina continued, "You wanta' blow some smoke, go ahead!" She struck a boxer's pose, arms up, presenting two underhand fists. "Come on, let's go!" Cassina danced in a semi-circle around the woman, sashaying back and forth.

The woman cowered like a rat, then broke, screaming and running all the way back to her car. She slammed the door and pulled out of the line of traffic. Brakes screeched as she performed a fast three-point turn and headed into traffic.

The sound of applause brought me up from my seat. From my vantage point, peering over the top of the steering wheel, I could see Cassina calmly give a tug at the waistband of her skirt, execute a tiny royal wave, and bow slightly to her public. She got in the car, saying nothing. I said nothing either, just handed her my handkerchief which she accepted.

"Jesus!" said Cassina.

"The bitch!" I said, without thinking, at once fearful that I had again gone too far.

Cassina was silent. She dabbed sweat from her forehead, paused for a moment, thinking, and finally shook her head in the affirmative. "Bitch," she said with authority.

We completed our errand with nothing more said about the incident. Cassina had glided into the appliance store, smiling and cooing, "How y'all doin' today? Hot, hot, hot! My, my!"

We headed downtown, laughing and cackling like chickens.

Chapter Three

"I'll Take My Stand"

THINKING ON IT now, that woman in traffic may have had some reason to be steamed and more reason than Cassina's showboating to feel afraid. It was a tense time.

Ten years before in Memphis, sanitation workers had gone on strike for sixty-five days. Martin Luther King had come to Memphis that April to support the strikers and was assassinated on a balcony of the Lorraine Motel, as you know. Riots had broken out and many people have told me about the awesome sight of National Guard tanks in the city's streets.

That summer of 1978, Memphis experienced again a tough round of municipal labor woes: On June 30, the fireman's union, presented with a "take it or leave it contract," left it. The next morning the firemen walked out, leaving the mayor having to call in one thousand National Guardsmen.

My roommate, Victor Braden O'Brien, and I sat, dumb-struck, watching the 10:00 news on television that night.

"I can't believe this is happening," he said.

"It's incredible. There, is that better?" I asked, adjusting the coat-hanger antenna.

"A little. What do they think they're doing?" he said, as images of a remote crew reporting from the scene of a fire flashed on the screen. "They're just standing there watching it burn!" An expensive-looking two story home rapidly became engulfed in flames.

"This shocking addition just in," the anchor interrupted. "Two firemen have just been arrested on charges of arson one block from the scene of a fire ... "

"What?" I yelled.

"Shh," said Braden, flagging me with his hand.

A man's face, captioned "Arson Suspect," filled the picture tube. "Yeah," he said stupidly, "I did it; I admit it."

"Do you believe this?" I had never seen Braden so incredulous.

Next up, came scenes from Overton Square, a restaurant and nightclub area in Midtown. Several old houses, now converted to apartments and shops, creaked and smoked, flames shooting from their upper stories.

"Holy shit!" I said, running to the back door of our house. An eerie, orange glow danced low in the summer sky to the south. We were less than a half a mile away.

The phone rang—Braden's father calling from Birmingham.

"Fine, yes," I heard Braden say.

Five minutes later, it rang again—this time, my mother back in Knoxville, only a shade shy of hysteria.

"We're fine ... no, nowhere near, really ... " I tried to sound casual. She sounded unconvinced. If she sounded it, I certainly felt it. "Nothing to worry about, Mother. Nothing at all."

In all, one-hundred-sixty-eight fires were reported that night. Sleep? Hardly.

The next morning's paper, in addition to the numerous reports of arson by firemen, reported also that several failing businesses, owned by individuals who, shall we say, "stood to gain" from their loss, conveniently had caught fire, too. But most shocking were the photographs of firemen in groups of fifteen or twenty who stood by, watching the blazes, some guzzling beer while they did.

The mayor imposed a 10:00 p.m. to 6:00 a.m. curfew the next day and the number of fires scaled back to about sixty. Seen on one street corner, a fireman bedecked in a toga, playing a violin. Around his neck, a sign with the name "Nero."

Our own circle from Dante's *Inferno* lasted four days before the strikers received a court order to return to work. Then, a federal mediator tried to work out a compromise for over a week. In fact, early that very morning that Cassina and I had lunched in Court Square—that day she had tried her best to induce me to auto-asphyxiation via Coca-Cola—the union rejected another "take it or leave it" offer by the city.

Two-hundred-thirty fires in those first three days of July, but my little home had been spared. Each day when I pulled into the driveway and saw the house, I felt deep kinship with Scarlett O'Hara viewing Tara through the mist. "It's still there!" I would cry out, rushing to the door, a victim of that same nervous kind of humor that makes people joke at funerals.

Tara it weren't—by a long shot. There are hundreds, thousands, of little bungalows like the one

Braden and I had rented throughout Midtown Memphis (the mid-town section of Memphis, is to its citizens, always capitalized as if it were a proper noun, a separate place: New York, Paris, Midtown), built in the Craftsman style of the 1910's - 1920's when the neighborhood was respectably fashionable, not funky, as the City of Memphis inched its way east from the river.

The original city was built along the Mississippi River, high on the bluffs, above the flood line. Someone once said that if downtown Memphis ever flooded, all of Arkansas (on the other side of the river) would be thirty feet under water. It was a smart move on the part of the founding fathers. Because of its situation, there was no place for Memphis to grow but north and east (Mississippi lay over the border to the south and there was some development there, but much of the area to the south of downtown, itself, was now either industrial or slum). The eastward choice was also a practical move, filling in the gap between town and the country estates that had been built as a refuge to a large degree from Yellow Fever epidemics which had almost wiped out the place, particularly one hundred years prior to the summer I now describe. Ah, anniversaries! But if Memphis had survived all that and more, I reasoned, surely a few score little ol' fires would be a small hurdle.

Aging houses as well as the flight further east after World War II (many times racially motivated—any Memphian will be honest enough to confess this to you), left a housing stock often snatched up by artistic types, musicians, and students like Braden and me from nearby Southwestern as well as the neighboring Art Academy. That's the changed and changing world we lived in, and to us, it was exciting (remember that we, ourselves, were very much "changed and changing," too, at that age). Anything and everything seemed possible.

So, not Tara, no, but five high-ceilinged rooms (six if you count the semi-enclosed front porch off the living room) on our floor. There was a closed-off stairway leading to a small apartment upstairs with its own separate entrance out back, this being occupied by a man I rarely saw (a med-student, as I recall, whose comings and goings did not dovetail with my own). We got the house from some seniors at the college who were moving. The owner/landlord had long ago retired, moved someplace in Mississippi, and happily rented the place to a steady stream of students for years, blissfully neglecting any maintenance all the while.

Between us, Braden and I had three pieces of furniture, including his recently acquired bed and my own: A hand-me-down from Mother and Dad. The rest of the furnishings were a *mish-mash* of styles—odds and ends left by our predecessors—which managed to supply everything we needed. Book shelves were the milk-crate kind—a standard student fixture for eons.

Judging from their condition, the walls had not been painted in twenty years, minimum. Their lack of freshness was overshadowed by an occasional pock-mark in the plaster which opened to reveal the wooden lathing underneath. One of these, on the ceiling in the living room, caught Braden's eye particularly. It was located just to the side of a bronze-colored, three-bulb light fixture in the Art Deco style. Throughout the angles and vertices of this minor monstrosity, someone had perched those inch-long plastic babies which used to come as premiums in some candy (Cracker Jack?) or like you get at Mardi Gras. Braden—ever the artist—thought the crack in the plaster resembled the female anatomy and threatened to paint a mural encompassing the entire birth-motif. I managed to dissuade him from the notion, arguing gamely that abstract minimalism was the order of the day; that *true* art lay in the unspoken concept, allowing the full *gestalt* to occur within the mind of the perceiver. To my complete amazement, he swallowed this line of complete hogwash and hung an original watercolor, a landscape, over the fireplace instead. I worried about him sometimes.

Worry, is precisely what the folks in Knoxville were doing. My parents had always been good about allowing me a certain degree of independence, but this experience of their only begotten living away from home an entire summer (although I had now completed two years in college) was new. Much later, I would recognize this as the natural stirrings of empty-nest syndrome. Had I been residing at the school, their fears would have been eased to some degree, with the knowledge of Alma Mater's watchful eye looking over me.

Both Dad and Mother called every day during the strike, urging me to come home, at least until things settled down. I stood my ground, though, and reluctantly they backed off. Were it not for the internship, I think they would have insisted.

It was not until several years later, reminiscing with them, that they would confess to me they had spoken to my faculty advisor by telephone about their concerns. The voice of a rational adult helped things along considerably.

"Rational adult," you will notice, is not a term I applied to myself. Was I? Who knows? You decide. Suffice it to say, I stayed.

"Rational" isn't an adjective easily applicable to *anything* that went on there the rest of the summer. Shortly after that bizarre incident involving the woman rapping on the car window, the real lunacy transpired.

On August 10, members of the Memphis Police Association, the union representing Memphis' finest, voted to reject their contract also and by midnight, began picketing station houses. The next morning, only seven hundred patrolmen and five detectives showed up for work throughout the entire city. County sheriff's deputies were assigned to patrol city streets while the National Guard was placed on alert. Again, the mayor imposed a curfew, this time beginning at 8:00 p.m. Throughout neighborhoods across the city, community patrols formed and housewives kept watch. Citizens prepared for the worst.

Ironically, (and I think there is something telling in this) the worst didn't happen. The overall crime rate actually dropped—forty percent. (Clearly, this was a place, as you will discover, where the expected thing didn't often occur.) Within the parameters of a city containing approximately 700,000 people, only two burglaries and one robbery were reported over the weekend. How could there be any crimes? Everyone stayed home.

Well ... almost everyone. The twisted lesson hidden in that statistic was wasted on some of us who had never before been in a situation like this. It was Braden who heard about a curfew party at Daffy's Saloon on Saturday night: Come early (before 8:00 p.m.), stay 'til 6:00 a.m.—leave at your own peril. The front door of the establishment was locked as curfew set in; windows shuttered. You see, the curfew only stipulated that, except for hospital and emergency personnel, no one could be on the streets between those hours. There was no law that said where one actually had to be.

The party lasted well past normal closing—who could arrest us?—and at least two young men, wheezing from cigarette smoke and so full of Tennessee sour-mash whiskey that they could have been labeled "combustible," made it until 4:00 a.m., when they snuck out a back door. Then they proceeded to creep stealthily across parking lots, down back alleys, and across the edge of a park, until at last they made it to North Parkway, a tree-lined boulevard running through Midtown, west towards downtown.

Like two little spies coming in from the cold, their mission was nearly complete. All that was left to do was cross the Parkway, sneak through another alley beside an apartment tower, hop a small chain-link fence, and cross an abandoned railroad spur until they came to their own backyard. Simple, no? That it appeared so to them is a testimony to their condition. (Not being fully aware of the statute of limitations on such crimes, I shall endeavor to keep these men's names secret, lest some zealous prosecutor somewhere seek to fulfill the letter of the law.)

They made it halfway across the six-lane road, stopping to rest in its landscaped median. One, an artistic type, seized the moment to begin pondering the splendor of the large tulip poplars which by day lent gentle shade to the lovely old street. As he admired the graceful curves of the branches, the other, a somewhat more reserved type, not possessed of the largest bladder that the Lord ever bestowed on a human being, announced forthrightly, "I gotta pee."

"So?" replied that artist, apparently enraptured by the tree he stood beneath, his tranquil contemplation interrupted only by a long, low burp rumbling up from his belly.

"Jeez," the other man said in response.

A perplexed look on the face of the first gave way to a slow grin—one part pride, two parts bourbon.

"Jeez!" the second man said again, this time with alarm. Rising out of the east were two headlights casting their bright beams in the man's direction.

"*Holy* Jeez," the artistic one said, his command of the vocabulary improving steadily.

"What'll we do?" the other man said, now beginning, as his need increased, to perform a quaint two-step.

Our two deer stood frozen for a moment as the headlights, coming from what appeared to be a jeep, came closer.

"The tree! Hurry!" The first man began to scamper up the one which moments before he had been worshipping. Following closely behind: The second man.

The jeep approached within two hundred feet. Just as it did, the second man slipped, catching himself on a branch. The first man, at once startled, then instinctively reaching down to help his friend, slipped, too, swung down, and hung fully upside-down by his knees for a moment. He managed to pull himself up until he caught the same branch with his hand. The second man dangled from an adjacent branch, four or five feet above the ground.

"Pretend you're invisible!" the first one, in a fit of snockered logic, whispered resourcefully.

"What!"

"Shut up!"

The jeep came to a halt fifteen feet from them. The door opened, and a Guardsman stepped out. He walked to the front of the vehicle; stopped, gazing ahead.

Turning, after a moment's contemplation, he walked back a few paces and stretched his camouflage covered arms over his head, taking in a deep breath as he did so. "Ahhhh," he said and struck a casual pose against the left side of the jeep.

In the tree, the inhabitants' arms began to ache. One, in particular, began to sweat. Profusely.

The guard fished for something in his breast pocket; withdrew a red box of Marlboros and a lighter. He lit one of the cigarettes and inhaled deeply, following up with an exhale of a large volume of smoke in one steady stream. He gazed vaguely in the direction of the tree, then turned his eyes heavenward, perhaps surveying a star or two that still hung in the smoky, pre-dawn sky. Such a lovely morning—why not pick this very spot to stop and enjoy it?

Meanwhile, back in the tree, a steady ache had set-in in the arms and shoulders of its occupants (to say nothing of the knees of one, the abdomen of another, as well as his feet which felt like lead weights hanging off the end of his blood-drained legs, and whose eyes, by now—so I am told—were both crossing and stinging, the sweat rolling into them off of his soaked forehead).

The guard finished his cigarette, tossed it to the pavement, and ground it out with an Elvis Presley-style back and forth twist of his boot.

Now, Memphis is a city just rich with musical heritage. Maybe it's just another of those odd things, but everyone there thinks he's a singer or a comedian or both, which I was to find out again and again in my time there. Before he left the two men, one to throw up and one to urinate so hard that he doubled over from the ache that spread through his nether lands—this guard decided to give a demonstration of his own particular talents.

He began slowly and gently—a veritable artiste he was—as the sky began to show the first signs of light and a warm and persistently determined wind wafted across the Parkway from the pachyderm house of the Memphis Zoo:

> " 'Aba, daba, daba, daba, daba, daba, dab,'
> said the Monkey to the Chimp.
> 'Baba, daba, daba, daba, daba, daba, dab,'
> said the Chimpie to the Monk ... ".

He went on throughout the song, opening the door of the jeep and finally performing a finish that would have made Jolsen proud before turning over the engine and driving away. The world was safe, once more, for democracy.

"THOSE GUYS" GOT off easily, because the following day, with over one thousand National Guardsmen patrolling, the Director of Police arrested forty people for violating curfew with twenty-six more added to the number by sunrise.

For my job, work went on as usual, with Cassina and me making our daily rounds. She reached over and snapped the knob of the car radio to "off."

"Sixty-six. Imagine that!" Cassina said, "and all cops!" The only people arrested had been picketing police officers.

"They're cracking down," I explained. "The mayor means to let them know he means business. He's threatened to fire 'em all if they don't go back in twenty-four hours."

"Business, schmizness," Cassina said, dismissing me and the mayor all by herself with one sweep of her hand. "That ain't gonna do no good."

"I don't know," I replied, "I heard that over at City Hall they're typing up the papers already and accepting applications for replacements."

"Never happen, never will." Cassina shook her head, adding a definitive, "unh-uh!"

We passed the newspaper building on our left and continued down Union Avenue. On the sidewalks, I noticed throngs of people.

"What do you mean, 'unh-uh'?"

"All the unions'll go out: "Teachers, newspapers, T.V.—who do you think those people are? They're all union. They can close down the whole port, too," she added.

A group of Asians carrying cameras disembarked from a charter bus pulled to the curb two blocks further along.

The prospect of what she was saying alarmed me. It seemed to me that the whole town could explode.

"Nobody wants that," Cassina assured me. "Oh, sure, they's always some nut out there who wants somethin' terrible, but I don' think anybody with sense wants that. People can remember things."

As we neared the old Hotel Tennessee, I again noticed something strange. We stopped for a red light, and a group of maybe two hundred people crossed the street in front of us.

"What *is* this?" I demanded. (I wondered if they were strike supporters.)

"Lord, Jackson," declared Cassina, "haven't you heard?"

"Heard what?"

"The king is dead!"

"King who?" Had some royal figure died? What did that have to do with Memphis? And *why* were all these people here?

"Where is he?" Cassina asked, looking around the car.

"He *who*?" I was lost again, an increasingly familiar state when I was with Cassina.

"He-*haw*, you mean," she said.

I was exasperated—"What are you talking about?"

"That mule!"

"Cassina! What mule?"

"The one that's done kicked you upside your head!"

"Aughhh!" I screamed, not caring who heard me.

The light changed; I stepped on the gas.

"Be careful!" She looked at the groups of people on the sidewalk. "You don't wanta kill nobody."

"Don't be too sure," I said, quickly fixing her with a look.

"The *king*, Jackson, the king!"

I still didn't get it.

"Elvis, dummy, Elvis!" She paused for a moment, dropped her head, and clucked her tongue. "Some day, they's gonna' run you outta this town on a rail! 'What king?' " she added scornfully.

"Well, I'm sorry! But ... "

"Don'tcha remember?" asked Cassina.

Suddenly it hit me. "He died ... "

" ... Exactly one year ago, day after tomorrow."

"Oh, my God ... " I looked out the window to witness a tiny Asian man snap a picture of a group standing in front of the Peabody Hotel. "Oh, my God."

"It ain't over 'til it's over," Cassina announced.

That day over thirty-thousand Elvis mourners poured into town; the firemen defied a court order and walked out again; meanwhile, the AFL-CIO considered a general strike.

Another curfew that night. Thirty firemen arrested, but fortunately, there were only a handful of fires, while the crime rate hit another low.

Then the lights went out.

It had cooled down to a comparatively frigid eighty-two degrees that evening and I could not sleep. On a work night, I usually tried to hit the sack by midnight, just after the Carson show. But that night, as I sat on the couch in front of the T.V., watching some creepy Bela Lugosi film on the Channel 3 Late Movie (with a fan in one hand and a can of Stroh's in the other), the picture tube and the lamp on the rickety end-table beside me went black simultaneously.

At first, I thought a fuse must have blown. (I was never too sure how the place was wired, anyway.) Fumbling for matches on the coffee table, my hand knocked over the fat orange and yellow Buddha candle that Braden had bought from a shop in the Square. Working blind, I managed to right the candle, tear a match from a book, and strike it. That's when I realized that something more was wrong. Ordinarily, if the lights were off in the living room, the spill from the street lamp was strong enough to cast shadows across the walls. The candle lit, I made my way to the door. Darkness.

Hesitating a second—this was eerie—I unlatched the screen door and kicked it open. From the steps, I could see very little that I was used to seeing. Slowly, my eyes began to adjust and solely with the aid of my candle and the natural light above, I scanned the horizon. Shapes only. Shapes in silhouette against the night sky.

A sharp pang struck within my gut. Nerves. No—*fear*—basic primoridial fear of the dark and the things that go bump therein.

"Sabotage," I whispered.

"DRUNKENESS," STATED THE morning paper's headlines, a little late, but on the stands nonetheless, correcting my assumption ten hours earlier. Apparently bored out of his mind as he stood watch at a power station, a security guard, assigned to prevent such occurrences as I feared, took to the bottle. Enchanted by the row of switches in front of him, he flipped one. A little while later, he flipped another. Then another. One by one—click, click, click—until he hit the lucky number seven, enough to plunge most of the city into darkness for three hours.

Cassina and I stood by a window in the 12th floor cafeteria at the bank, gazing down onto the mall where thousands of tourists clad in t-shirts emblazoned with pictures of big, broken red hearts and "Long Live the King" streamed past striking policemen and firemen.

"This is too much," I said.

" 'Deed it is," she agreed, scanning the paper. "Look, it says here that three students were treated for elk-bite at a hospital last night."

"You're making that up."

"No, I'm not!" she protested, handing the paper to me. "See for yourself."

Before I had time to look, she said, "See there, three students snuck into the zoo last night to party, an' got bit by a elk."

There it was in print before me.

"It's like being in a Fellini film," I said, looking back out at the crowds below.

"Fellini? Never cared for it—gives me gas."

"You missed," I told her. "Badly."

"Guilty as charged."

"I don't get it," I said (meaning the labor situation).

"No, you don't," Cassina agreed.

"What?"

"Well, jus' look at it, Jackson. How much money is involved here?"

"Two-hundred-fifty-thousand dollars. That's what the news said." The contract dispute involved a total of two-hundred-fifty-thousand dollars in increased wages. "That's a lot of money."

"No, it ain't," she argued.

The Business Math major in me rushed forward in defense: "Well, it is when they're trying to cut costs, balance a budget, and avoid a deficit!"

"Phooey!"

"Phooey, yourself."

"Jackson, look at me. Now all those National Guard out there, where you think they's comin' from?"

"I don't know."

"From our pockets, that's where!" she said. "Whattaya reckon all that's costin'?"

I had never thought about it.

"Well, accordin' to Mr. Meyerman ... an' I reckon a man like that knows what he's talkin' about ... " she said, " ... the bill for that service rendered is 'bout seventy-thousand dollars a day."

"No!"

"Yes! Wake up!" Cassina put her hand on my shoulder—she rarely touched me for some reason, so I paid attention. "Look over there." She pointed to the memorial for Martin Luther King across the Mall. "See where those policemen are?"

Several hundred men had gathered beneath the memorial.

" 'sfunny, ain't it?"

I shook my head, confused.

"Where'd'ya think all them fellas was ten years ago?"

"I don't know."

"On the other side," she said. "Arrestin' strikers."

"Some, sure. Some not."

"True," she said, conceding, "but ain't it funny?" Then she said something else that surprised me. "My husband got hisself killed, then."

"I'm sorry. I didn't know."

"No."

That was the first time Cassina ever mentioned anything about that part of her life.

"Cassina," I said, "what's all this about?"

She chose a quote to answer me:

" 'And they said to one another, Behol',
this dreamer cometh. Come now therefore,
'n' cast him into some pit, 'n' we will say,

Some evil beast hath devoured him: 'n' we
shall see what will become o' his dreams.' "

In all her myriad mysterious moments, I never before or never after witnessed her so mysterious, so mystical as this. It was the most deeply political thing I ever heard her utter. And the most Biblical.

Before it was over, two days later, one-hundred-thousand fans of Elvis Presley had descended, the temperature had topped one hundred degrees, more police were arrested as more firemen refused to fight fires. And the City of Memphis spent over one million dollars for the services of the National Guard.

Chapter Four

"Night Of South Winds! Night Of The Large Few Stars! Still Nodding Night! Mad Naked Summer Night!"
—Walt Whitman
"Songs of Myself"

IT HAD BEEN a summer of firsts: Anniversaries of deaths, college boys away from home for the season, eccentrics met, elk bites treated, strikers of the "bravest" and "finest" ... and it was almost over.

"Whatcha' got planned for Labor Day?" Cassina asked me one day in the car.

"I'm not completely sure about that, yet. But, tonight, I've got a date."

Cassina perked up, "Oh, well now ... Who with?"

"Regina Ann Fitzwater," I replied.

"Oh," said Cassina with clearly waning interest. Obviously, she did not approve, because for the rest of the trip she said nothing, just looked around the car and out the windows, head bobbing like one of her famous pigeons. I was tempted to point this out to her, but refrained. Cassina puckered her lips a little and clicked at her fingernails every so often as we drove on without saying anything more. She had already said it all.

THAT NIGHT I lost my virginity to Regina Ann Fitzwater. There had been a long list of tasks for me to accomplish over the course of the season; this was the last on my personal list. At twenty, I suspected it was time to take the plunge, so to speak. Despite all the bravado talk in the dorms at Southwestern, I'm fairly sure that I was not the only male who had yet to experience the full joys of the flesh.

Sex was very much talked about on campus, of course, and the environment was a progressive one, to say the least. You must remember that this was the late 1970's—a time wedged between the Vietnam counter-culture and the onset of the AIDS epidemic. Men and women students lived openly with each other off campus and only a little less openly (for it was not officially sanctioned by the college) on the grounds.

The buzz was that there was experimentation of the male/male, female/female type going on. Who knows? Maybe it was all a fraternity prank. Or maybe it was a group of people eager to know as much about themselves and their sexuality as they did about Aquinas, Keats, and Quantum Physics. Nevertheless, such things were discussed with an amazing amount of sophistication. I'm often amazed at today's supposed "openness". Do kids today think that they've just invented sex?

Being a small community, secrets were difficult to keep. I rather enjoyed being of the *cognoscenti* (or seemingly so), but then, as now, appreciated the value of "privacy." (That may be the old Knoxville conservatism battling from within.) Looking back on it, there were many "activities" at the college, but the reality was probably somewhat less than the appearance to me at the time. My being twenty and eager colored my vision, as did my being twenty and relatively new to such exposure. In the clarity of hindsight, as I think of several classmates, either they were extraordinarily discreet or else in the same predicament as I. Traditional morals clashed with new freedoms, naturally, but ours was a group definitely eager to explore fully in the newfoundland of the Sexual Revolution. Which is a clever way of saying that, in short, we were a randy little lot.

MY OWN PARTICULAR deflowering occurred on an island in the Mississippi River on the Thursday night before Labor Day, 1978. It was then or never, so I thought—if indeed I did actually do any real *thinking* in my hormonally intoxicated state. With my internship at the bank set to end the next day and with school scheduled to resume in nine days—nine days which mostly would be spent by me back in Knoxville—I knew that classes and college-related activities (the legitimate kind) would keep me from seeing Regina Ann Fitzwater. I was, admittedly, a cad. She was, though, admittedly, not the type of girl to wait. I was right pleased to know this.

I use the term "girl" when I speak of her, but Regina Ann Fitzwater was actually an "older woman" by five years. She worked at the bank and was rumored to be having an affair with a married executive in the accounting department. Needless to say, lust, pure and unbridled, had knocked any sense I may have once possessed right out of my head.

It all began with a little flirtation just two weeks before and on this, our second date, it would end not with a whimper. Following a dinner at a bistro in Overton Square, we decided to take a drive. Now Regina lived with her parents in a neighborhood near the airport, but I, as you know, shared a house with Braden not far from campus, which was just a short drive through the park, three blocks from the square. What? Five minutes away? It occurred to me that we could easily have gone there, but this being my first time, I wanted to make sure it was memorable. Sex in an automobile is a cliché; it is also *really* uncomfortable. It must have been nervousness that made me so stupid, and the desire for privacy (no roommates lurking). A car parked on an island seemed perfectly fine at the time. Okay, give me a break....

At dinner, I casually asked Regina Ann, "May I have a roll, please?" From the moment she lazily stroked the back of my hand, I knew that I was going to get one. Three times after that, I almost knocked over my water glass, but thankfully managed not to. Jittery. It was like being a kid at the circus waiting to see the big cats. The ones with teeth.

With trembling hands, I escorted Regina Ann to my old Toyota and we headed downtown towards the river.

Mud Island, where we were going, is aptly named. Starting around 1900, it began to rise just off shore from the northern part of downtown Memphis, formed by deposits of mud that built up about where the much smaller Wolf River empties into the grand confluence of waters that is the Mississippi River.

At the time of my visit with Regina Ann, there was nothing on the island save a tiny unkempt park on the northern end, reachable by way of a small road that had been built by the Army Corps of Engineers to connect it to the mainland.

Few people knew of this park for some reason, or if they knew, did not visit it. I had been there twice before that night, but in the daytime, taken by a college buddy, a Memphis native who knew every nook and cranny of the city. Rarely did I see another vehicle the times I had visited it before or since.

The view from the island was spectacular. To the north, the wide open spanse of the river snaking along its course. To the west, a row of zelkovas shooting up out of the steep bank of the island before it plummeted into the water. Beyond the river, lay the fertile flood plains of Arkansas. And to the east and south, the ancient cobblestones leading out of the water and up the riverbank to the warehouses and towers of the city of Memphis, rising proudly on the fourth Chickasaw bluff.

Crossing over the island, high in the air, soared the green arcs of the Hernando DeSoto Bridge—the "Big M" as it is called for its great twin arches which mimic the bends of the river below and also form the initial of the city whose very existence derived from that river. The hum and swoosh of cars and trucks passing overhead from downtown to West Memphis and points beyond reminded me of the sound I once heard in a Biology class, listening through a stethoscope to the rush of blood through arteries as we checked our blood pressure. The southern tip of Mud Island is now home to a river museum, a park and amphitheatre all accessible via sky-tram from downtown. I do not know exactly what development has taken place on the northern end, or even if the little park of my memory is still there.

There is exactly where we found ourselves, though, that night—Regina Ann Fitzwater and myself.

Amazingly, (and irritatingly enough) sex was *not* the only thing on my mind at that moment. At dinner, we had run into a professor at the college whose course in Religion I would be taking that fall (having already signed up for it the previous spring). She was a sturdy woman, this professor, with jet-black hair somewhat severely brushed back, revealing a formidable widow's peak. She had a friendly smile, though, and as she shook my hand, she mentioned warmly that she looked forward to getting to know me in class.

I had suppressed a giggle when she said that, because in my state, anticipating that which was to come, I had been unable to avoid the unfortunate association of "getting to know" someone and its connotation in the Bible. With Regina Ann just waiting there ripe for "knowing" and me oh-so-ready for the "knowledge," the connection was almost more than I could bear. (It's the innocent remark that will get you every time.) I gnawed the inside of my lower lip.

Had I not been so determined to appear suave and experienced to Regina Ann, perhaps I would have shared my semi-naughty thought with her in the car and we would have had a good laugh. That would have been the end of it—steam diffused. As it was, though, my attempt at suppression only kept the subject of religion coming to mind.

To get to the island by way of the secret back road, we had to drive through an area of town known to some as the Pinch, where the large Jewish community of Memphis had first gathered. Not a good start. Visions of pogroms and scenes from *Fiddler on the Roof* flashed through my brain. Next, naturally, followed idol worship, golden calves, and divine retribution.

All of this did nothing to allay my basic fears which were that, with all the anticipation and excitement of "the first time," I would either perform too quickly or panic and not be able to act at all.

The late summer heat did not help much either. Nor did the mosquitoes which inevitably flew in the necessarily opened windows of the compact car we sat parked in.

I kissed Regina Ann and she moaned softly. Hands began to explore and arms tangled. From the river, we heard a tow boat's horn as it slo-o-o-wly pushed a barge up river. My hand, which had been resting on her thigh, slo-o-o-wly began to travel under her skirt.

But, then there was that thing—that *Bible* thing—rearing its ugly head. Was it guilt? Was it God laughing at his two ridiculous creatures contorting themselves in the small car below?

Nervousness and fear are not conducive to good sex. Neither are heat, mosquitoes, and automobiles. But perhaps the cruelest saltpeter of all is early religious training coupled with a phenomenal memory and a vivid imagination.

"Bring them out unto us, that we may know them," the Sodomites cried out in my mind.

Next up, my childhood Sunday School teacher spoke: *"And God said unto him in a dream, ... I know that thou didst this in the integrity of thy heart; for I also withheld thee from sinning against me; therefore suffered I thee not to touch her."*

And now a guest appearance from the severe-haired professor, *"Adam knew Eve his wife, and she conceived."*

Conceived? Whoops! "Oh, my God!"
"Yes, baby, oh yes!" said Regina.
Baby? Baby! No baby, oh no. Not a baby! Please!

"And the Lord said, I have seen the affliction of my people and know their sorrows."

"No!" I shouted, trying to clear away the images in my mind.

Regina looked confused. "No?"

"Uh ... no," I parried, moving her hand to a more strategic location, "no, touch me there instead." *My sword must needs be mightier than all their pens.*

"Mmmm," groaned Regina as she opened her mouth to me.

"Mmmm," I replied before leaning down to take it.

Must not think, I told myself. *Must concentrate on something else. That's the ticket!* My hands were under her skirt, removing her silk panties. Hips wriggling, she helped me along.

Another image: The walls of Jericho tumbling. Destruction. Charlton Heston throwing down the Ten Commandments.

Do something, for God's ... No! Do something! What? A plan: Be someone else. Someone ... Anyone! Anything to override the Cecil B. DeMille epic reeling its way through my mind. Temples crumbling. Wheels flying off chariots. *Help!*

Now, it is written, "ask, and ye shall receive." And so, I looked, and lo! the answer was right there in my hand. No, the other one. For Regina Ann Fitzwater, in her mysterious way, had sewn a laundry tag just beneath the elastic waistband of her store-bought drawers. I performed a double-take worthy of an Olympic medal. The tag read, "Property of R.A.F."

"R.A.F." Images of destruction and divine wrath ground to a halt. The reel changed and suddenly, there I was, born anew as Ronald Coleman, starring in my own feature. I, the dashing hero, flying a dangerous mission for the Crown. I had my orders, understood the task before me. Must get the precious serum through. Not just for me—no, no!—but for the good of England, for the honour of the men in the Force. Yea, verily, for all men everywhere!

Me, a noble fighter for the R.A.F. I looked down at the landing strip beneath me in the moonlight. How many flyboys had landed their equipment there before me? No, mustn't think of that now. Must think of duty.

I swatted a mosquito off my neck. *Damn! The enemy will stop at nothing, nothing I tell you! The bloody bastards! Vicious, conniving bastards!*

I looked down to see her there. *Yes, yes! It is her, the fair Pamela, pride of all Britain, gamely waving me in.*

"Hello!" I call down to her.

"Hello!" she says back, laughing.

I can see the hangar, doors open. Darkness all around. *Must make it there. Must. I must deliver.*

Pamela is calling: "Yes! Now, yes! Hurry!"

Mustn't stop now. Hand on the throttle, butt to the wind. I bear down and land, easing gently, effortlessly into Pamela's hangar. Victory is mine! And all for king and country. I cry out: " 'Tis a far, far better thing I do than I have ever done before!"

"Whudjewsay?"

Long after my propellers had stopped spinning, I sat there, arm around Regina, in that car, on that funny little island that had appeared out of nowhere, and gazed out into the black Arkansas sky. Back to my senses. The summer had been a good one. Sure, I know: A corny old sentimental thought, you bet. But I'd be wrong in trying to tell you that I was anything other than corny old sentimental me.

THE NEXT DAY at work proved uneventful for the most part. Several people were not in owing to the long Labor Day weekend. That was good, because I looked like refried hell.

It had been well after three when I arrived at my home from returning Regina to hers. Braden's door was closed so I could not share the night's triumph with anybody else. Too bad. It's hard to remember much else except removing my wrinkled clothes and flopping onto my unmade bed.

Morning slapped me in the face like its honor had been insulted. Looking at myself in the mirror, I sure knew why.

Cassina eyed me suspiciously when I picked her up at the Meyerman home Out East later that morning, but made no comment. She was oddly quiet I thought as we drove, especially since this was to be my last day of interning and I didn't know really when we would see each other again.

The group that I worked with had kindly invited to take me out for a farewell lunch, so I would be eating later than usual that day. Because of that, and because of my bleary-eyed state from the previous night's escapades, I made my way to the break room on the 12th floor where there were vending machines for soft-drinks and candy as well as coffee. Despite the hung-over feeling I had, I was actually rather contented as I walked down the plushly carpeted hall.

I gave the heavy wooden door a smack and it swung open. Cassina was there, sitting at a small round table directly across from the entranceway.

"Hey!" I said sportily. No one else was in the room.

"Hey, yourself," she shot back.

I dropped a quarter into the vending machine and pressed the button for a packaged doughnut. Maybe sugar would boost the old energy level.

Cassina, sitting by the window, began to hum a little tune.

A dime in those days would buy me a six-ounce stryofoam cupful of delicious, old-fashioned, machine-made, coffee-colored liquid. As the cup was filling, I could hear over the buzz and trickle that she was singing now—kind of sweet and low-like. She was up to something ....

The machine stopped and I removed the cup, set it on the formica counter, and turned to the refrigerator for milk.

"Getting to know you, getting to know all about you," she intoned in her saloon baritone.

I swung around. "What's that supposed to mean?" Milk sloshed from the container.

"My goodness," she said, stopping abruptly. "Somebody's awfully jumpy today! I'm just singin', that's all."

I eyed her sternly. Cassina, I knew too well already, never "just" did anything. "Okay." I turned back around and poured a half-ounce of milk into my coffee, capping the jug and returning it to the fridge when I was through. Leaning over to pull a paper towel from the metal dispenser so that I could clean up the spill, I heard it again. The humming.

As I finished cleaning and stuffed the paper towel through the swinging door of the trash can, the humming grew louder till it reached its zenith and she broke into full-throated song, "Haven't you no-ticed? Suddenly I'm bright and bree-e-e-zy."

I glared at her.

She now sang staccato, like a mouse tiptoing—"Be-cause of - all - the - bea-u-tiful and new" (a slow crescendo) "things I'm learning about you" (the big finish) "Day, by ... "

"All right! All right!" I bellowed, "That's enough!"

She giggled.

"What's got into you?" I demanded.

"Me?" she feigned innocence. "Me?" she repeated. "Nothin'. Nothin's got into me. Not me. No, sir." The little snort she added was a deft touch.

"All right then."

And it would have been, too, had she not said the next thing. "Why, I'm not the one going around the place looking like the cat that ate the pussy!"

"You know! Don't you? You know! How could you ... "

Cassina dissolved in laughter. She howled and hooted then fell over the tabletop, pounding it with her fist.

"Cassina! Cassina Gambrel, you look at me!" She did. "Cassina, stop looking at me!"

More guffaws from her.

"All right, that's enough! Who told you? Who? Was it Regina Ann?"

"Regina Ann!" Cassina feigned shock and horror. "No, I promise. I haven't heard a word from Regina Ann. Cross my part an' hope to die." She drew a quick "x" on her chest.

"Well, then, who?"

"Jackson Taylor, what are you talkin' about?"

Suddenly, I could feel the heat in my face, the color rising, my ears warming. "Cassina!"

No use, she was gone again. Gales, torrents of laughter. Snorts and snickers. Finally she gasped, recovered a bit, and looked at me. "I got to go," she said. "This is too much. *You're* too much." She got up from the table and crossed to the door, launching into her full-throated reprise: " ... Getting to like you. Getting to hope you like ... " (pause) " ... me."

"Cassina, life is not a musical comedy, you know.... "

" ... suddenly I'm bright and bree-zy."

"Not everything's a song cue for you, Cassina."

"Because of all - the - bea-ut-ti-ful and new ... "

"Very funny, Cassina. Ha. Ha."

" ... learning about you ... "

"Don't do it, Cassina ... "

Perfectly in time with the music—that woman had been trained by the pros—she opened the door and waltzed through.

" ... by day!"

"Cassina Gambrel, you come back here!"

But the door closed and she was gone.

Chapter Five

"Cassina Gambrel Is Missing"

"CASSINA GAMBREL IS missing." That is what the letter said. It was a double-surprise, that letter, because it was from Braden O'Brien, who, I assumed, after fifteen years, I would not hear from again and because it contained that shocking sentence that leapt off the page:

> "I know that we parted on a bad note, but
> also knew instinctively that this bizarre
> turn was something you should be informed
> of—Cassina has, it seems, disappeared."

Stunned, I sat there for what seemed like an hour, but a glance at the clock confirmed only two minutes. All time seemed to warp. All memories now took on a different perspective—clicked into a different frame of reference entirely upon this news.

> "The police have been notified and are
> searching everywhere. It seems odd to
> ask if by chance you may have seen her.
> An investigation by the authorities of her
> home gives no indication that she had set
> out to travel. I am afraid to say that I

fear the worst. Am trying to keep my chin up.

"Should you choose to come here, now or in the immediate future, I'm certain that many people would be glad of your company in this difficult time. My address is still as above, or telephone me at the studio or home."

The letter went on to give the two telephone numbers, one of which I recognized as the same number we had in college. The address, too, in black at the top of the page was the same Midtown one for the house we had shared. My fingers glided over the script. "Engraved," I said aloud. And, heavy on the sarcasm, "Well, la-di-da, Mr. O'Brien." After all these years, I hoped that he had put at least as much care into his house as he had his stationery, else, surely it would be a pile of rubble by now. No doubt, a pile of rubble with plastic Mardi Gras babies on top.

I lit a cigarette and walked to the living room window. Gray sky hovered low. Snow on the way. About a foot of it lay on the ground already; more piled up around the telephone poles and against the curbs as far down the steep hill as I could see from there. Turning back to the room piled high with books and papers in the corners, beside the tables, on the tables, etc., etc., I decided to ignore the fact that my apartment was a dump not too much better than Braden's place.

I found the telephone under the previous day's *Boston Globe* and punched in the numbers with my thumb. What else could I have done?

Two rings. "Heh-lo?" The voice was softer than I remembered, low, slowly dragging the first syllable as if it were an unruly child being pulled along by the hand.

I cleared my throat. "Braden?"

"Jackson Taylor" we both said together. Realizing what had happened, I said, "Yes."

A pause. "How are you, Jackson?"

Oh, just ducky! "Fine. And you?" *We're going to be sociable? . . . Whattya think—I called to chat?*

"Fine. Well, . . . " He hesitated.

"I got your letter. I, uh, I'm glad you wrote," I said somewhat awkwardly.

"Good," said the voice on the phone, followed by more silence.

"What's going on, Braden? What is all this?"

"She's missing," he said and I detected, for the first time, a distraught tone in his voice which had been absent from his peculiarly formal letter and which caused me some alarm. "No one knows a thing about her whereabouts. I was hoping . . . "—he broke off.

"No," I jumped in. "I'm sorry. I haven't heard anything. Not a word."

"Come to Memphis," he said suddenly.

"What?"

"Come to Memphis," he repeated. "It's crazy. I know. Maybe ... "

There was such an urgency there now that, automatically, I went on the defensive. "Oh, come on!" I want to say, but instead: "I have classes, Braden. I teach; I just can't ... "

"I know. It was stupid. I'm sorry."

"Forget it," I said. *This was a mistake.*

There was a long, awkward pause.

"Jackson ... "

Whatever it was, I wasn't ready to hear it, didn't *want* to hear it. I cut him off roughly. "Thank you for letting me know, Braden."

"I thought you would want to."

"I appreciate it."

Another pause. This time it was broken by me. "I have to go."

"Jackson, I ... "

"I have to go," I said sharply. He was silent and after a moment, I added, "Keep me posted, will you?"

"Right-o."

My finger found the disconnect button and pressed.

IF THAT EPISODE has not disabused you of any notions that I am some sort of saint, let me firmly state: I am not. Neither was Braden. Cassina wasn't either. Nobody is. Cassina was Cassina and that is that.

As a matter of fact, let's just stop right here. And yes, if I sound angry it is because I *am* angry with you if you are doing any of us the disservice of making us stock characters or stick-figures representational, in your limited view, of the heroic figures of the land known as the South, the people that dwell therein, or those possessed of its mind. Yes, its mind. How dare you! Come to think of it, I'm downright furious with you. I've half a notion to go no further with you, to leave you stranded right here, beached as you are on a sandbar of ignorance, with the currents swelling perilously all 'round, and say to you, "Swim or stay put!"

Cassina was no Mammy, no Rosa Parks, either. Get it out of your head. She was a mystery to me and I

knew that long ago.
   But you're wondering what happened ....

   THE YELLOW PAGES were in a stack underneath a pile of magazines which all toppled over and slid halfway across the living room floor when I tugged at the book. I cursed and kicked at them before thumbing through to the "Airlines" section. I found the number of one, dialed it, and booked a ticket out for two days later. The next call was to a Memphis hotel; the third to Benjamin Tilman, the head of the department at the small community college where I taught.
   "Ben, it's Jackson Taylor."
   "Jackson—how are you?"
   "Not so well I'm afraid, Ben."
   "What is it? What's wrong?"
   "Cassina Gambrel is missing."
   Explaining to Ben exactly who Cassina was and why I felt compelled to leave my job that Thursday afternoon in order to travel fifteen-hundred miles, miss four days of teaching on only two days notice with the strong possibility of jeopardizing my job in the process, was at best a daunting task. Cassina was neither a relative nor was she a close friend any more (fifteen years without speaking will have an amazing way of doing that).
   In his skillful and subtle way, Ben questioned my sanity. I believe his exact words were, "Are you out of your fucking mind?"
   "There's a good possibility, Ben."
   "Come on, Jax, what gives?"
   "Cassina Gambrel is missing." He'd offered a graceful exit; I'd ignored it. *No turning back now, huh?*

"She's the one ... You told me about her once; I remember now. Something about catering a party ... "

"Yes, that's right, Ben. That's the one."

"And that crazy summer with all of those tourists...." Ben had a good memory of my cocktail party repertoire.

"Right, right, right."

"And ...?"

"She's missing."

"But Jax, a week ... "

"Not a week, four days. I don't teach on Fridays. I have nothing on the weekend. There are no committees."

"She's not a family member?"

"No." A gulp washed down the huge embarrassment.

He hesitated. "And this is very important to you?"

"Very," I said—a wing and a prayer. Waited. Waited more.

"Okay."

I found myself exhaling audibly and felt a tight stitch in my gut. It wasn't until then that I realized the amount of tension this sudden ordeal caused me.

"When can I count on your being back here?" Tilman asked.

"Sunday evening next. I promise," I said.

"Class on Monday morning, right?"

"Right." *Absolutely. Anything you say.* My ass was on the line big-time. "Thanks, Ben."

"You're welcome, Jax. I hope everything works out all right."

"Thank you."

"I'm not sure I understand this ..." he said before hanging up the telephone.

What was not to understand? Cassina Gambrel was missing.

THE NEXT FORTY-EIGHT hours were a whirlwind of telephone calls to students in my day classes as well as the one evening section I taught, frantic packing of suitcases, calls to neighbors asking for assistance with mail and newspaper pick-up, an arrangement with the kid next door to feed Priscilla the cat, and mammoth anxiety.

Fifteen years before, I drove away from Memphis, Tennessee thinking never to return. There had been a Christmas card or two exchanged with some individuals over the years, the alumni newspaper which seven years ago I started reading out of curiosity, and an occasional column about the city clipped from the newspaper and tucked into an envelope by an old colleague or friend, but basically, that was it. Family obligations took me to Knoxville on occasion. However, I could see no reason to make the trek further west. Avoidance. Our tenth class reunion had come and gone; I sent regrets—it conflicted with some meeting, some conference. Best wishes. Here's a check.

Here I was in Boston, so very different than Memphis. So like Memphis. Much smaller within the city proper, much older, much more rooted in tradition, much more ethnocentrism. Much, much, much ... so much more restrictive in some ways, so much freer in others in terms of expectations. Ah, hell! Who am I kidding? They are so *very* alike, only with a different cast of characters. I had moved over fifteen-hundred miles away, but hadn't budged an inch. Because as I was to find out soon enough, it's all dependent on the perspective of the viewer and this one had progressed very little in all those years.

IT WAS A long flight. Turbulence outside New York set my already queasy stomach churning and I thought for a good half-hour that I might actually be ill. Some cold water splashed on my face in the cramped plastic and chromium restroom helped. The greenish fluorescent light under whose flicker I viewed myself in the mirror did not. There is something rather sickening, too, about that recycled, re-chilled air that streams from that never-quite-correctly-adjustable little plastic nozzle above one's airplane seat that always reminds me of a dentist's office: Sterile and efficient, not comfortable or comforting.

At last we approached Memphis. Images assaulted me through the scratched glass window: Rows and rows and rows of houses springing up out of the landscape like strange crops; the old water tower in Germantown; tall buildings Out East—some I did not recognize—*What a surprise—where did you come from?*; the long, familiar east-west traffic arteries, predictably clogged. The wing dipped. Below me, Memphis State University—*huge*.

For whatever reasons pilots do these things, we continued west, past the airport—*Good Lord, they haven't moved it, have they?*—and flew downtown. *All these new buildings!* tall and modern around the old ones I knew, had driven to or past. *Oh! No. That's over there—not next to that!*—my memory correcting itself. A gigantic pyramid structure. The sun glinted off it and I shielded my eyes for a moment. The river—a demented blue-green snake.

The plane banked and we were in our final descent, back to the airport. Me, like a kid again—gawking, rubber-necking. That only made me think of Cassina.

Memphis International is on the south side of town, just north of the Mississippi line. Flat land. Miles of it. We taxied forever to the gate and I overheard someone telling the old joke about Memphis being the largest city in Mississippi and something about planes actually landing down in Jackson then driving the rest of the way. God, it seemed like it. Feels worse when you're alone. Worse still when you find yourself feeling, suddenly and uncomfortably, as vulnerable as an eighteen year old in a strange land, but with the experience of a thirty-seven year old who knows it ain't all grand, feeling not at all at ease with being once more child-like.

It had often been my experience to disembark at the farthest gate in the huge, Y-shaped terminal and lucky me, guess what? Welcome home!

Ten minutes later, I arrived at the main area. As I stepped on the escalator to go down to the baggage claim, my head tilted up, viewing the vast, vaulted ceiling above. I was in a daze.

Luggage claimed. Car rented. A perky clerk with a shoulder-length, chestnut-colored mane that flipped up at the ends asked me if I needed anything else. My eyes dropped to the space above her left breast where her nametag had been pinned—a parallelogram roughly approximating the shape of the state in robin's egg blue. The white letters etched into it read:

"Hello!
My name is
Peggy-Lynn."

Beneath that, on a separate decal stuck to her uniform, black lettering on a red background queried in its best cursive:

"May I help you?"

Not a chance, Peggy-Lynn. I'm past it.
"Mister Taylor?" Peggy-Lynn called me from the fog. "Mister Taylor?"
"What?" Then shaking my head, hoping to clear it, "I'm sorry."
"Will you be needin' anything else?"
"Sorry. Disoriented a little." I felt the need to explain somehow. "It was a long flight."
"Oh, I understand, Mister Taylor, it's okay."
This was a far cry from car rental in Boston. Maybe it was the accent, the accents, now unfamiliar, swarming all around me like ... what? ... bees, I guess is the simplest simile to convey it—so far from the harsh emphasis of the Boston brogue on the first syllable of my name—"Taye" —and the broad "a" sound that clipped the "o-r" right from the end—"Taye-lah" whenever I transacted business of any kind in Boston, including "high-reen a cah."
Peggy-Lynn smiled sweetly.
I caught myself half-staring, then returning the smile. "Everything's fine. Thank you."
"Do you know where you're goin'?" Peggy-Lynn offered a map.

Not in the least. "Yes, I think so. Midtown. I used to live here, long ago." *You were probably two years old.* "It's Airways to East Parkway, East Parkway on into Union or maybe Poplar, right?"

"That's it!" she chirped.

"Great!" I chirped right back. "Now, which way?"

Peggy-Lynn gave me a wilted look.

"I mean to the car."

"Oh!" She perked right back up like a daisy. "Just through that door and across the drive. Follow the signs."

I smiled at her and stooped to pick up my bags. "Thank you."

"Thank *you*, Mister Taylor," she said, "and welcome home."

"Thanks." Behind the new smile I gave her, I swallowed hard. *What is this I'm feeling?*

DRIVING THOSE STREETS again proved odd. I knew the way, although after all this time, certain sites had changed. Daffy's Saloon, where, following classes on many a late afternoon, so many of the world's more pressing crises were scrupulously analyzed then subsequently solved in that naive way that only college students, full of hope and bursting at the seams with new theories, do, had ceased to be. The old building had been razed leaving a rubble-strewn lot. As insignificant as a change like that may seem, the shift leaves a peculiar feeling of loss in the pit of one's stomach. Time has passed. Things have changed. And a visible symbol exists to crack any attempts at denial, rendering them futile. But the way came back automatically, although the entire trip seemed to move in a hallucinatory slow motion—some distorted film viewed through gauze.

I arrived at the hotel across from the Peabody Library in Midtown. The location was chosen because it was in the most familiar territory I knew. Despite my trepidation at being back in Memphis, something wanted to be safe, comfortable. I know—it was, that feeling weird already, I didn't want to be more discombobulated by being in *terra incognita*. Keep my feet on a known route. The sensation of operating on automatic pilot might prove an advantage. Instinct could perhaps guide me to Cassina Gambrel.

Check-in was easy—Keys handed over by a young woman, about twenty, whose lips parted to reveal two large front teeth when she delivered her professional smile. The name on her tag said, "Marebeth Trotwell." I was back.

Upstairs, I flopped on the bed, sinking quickly into a dream that I was on some sort of a boat. I tell this to you now in the same vivid images that appeared to me from the deepest, weirdest, recesses of my sub-conscious mind. All right: Put yourself in my position. You're on a boat somewhere in the Atlantic. In England, they are loading the Queen Mother into a canon. Meanwhile, in Hyanisport, Mrs. Kennedy is being strapped into a catapult.

They tamp down Her Majesty good and proper and light the fuse. Mrs. K says a rosary and the cable is readied.

Bam and thwang!

You look up in time to see just what it is that happens when an irresistible force meets an unstoppable object.

The amalgam produced lands on a Walking Horse in an arena where a brass band is playing "When the

Saints Go Marching In." Suddenly, the horse bucks and bolts, throwing its rider. And the thing that fell to earth is Cassina Gambrel.

See, I told you anything could happen.

Chapter Six

"A Modern-Day Icarus"

THE BELL TOWER at Southwestern is an imposing structure which can be seen from a distance rising above the ancient oaks of the campus and surrounding area. At night, it is flooded with white light streaming from instruments beneath, angled upward as if they are the heads of worshipers craning to see their god; each of the particles emanating from them a tender caress against the cool, smooth skin of its limestone and the sensuously graceful curves of its gothic arches.

There, there, there it stands—"a joy forever"—pointing as if to say, "No, I am not; look again. I point to the One who is."

The massive clapper strikes like a fist below the belt of the bell that is suspended there. Its tone a fist in a velvet glove. The sonorous sound a slap back to the reality which appears equally suspended, suspended, suspended in the dizzying beauty. The cheeks of that beauty receive the assaults that land every half-hour and even more vigorously on the hour—a tattoo. On grand occasions—a convocation, a commencement—the sound resonates splendidly against the soul of its students. At deaths, its vibrato rolls out a mourning chant, "All that you see is not all that is. Remember. Remember ... "

Above it, a bird, a cloud, or a sky: fiercely blue in autumn, gray as a dove in winter, and bright as a baby's eyes in the spring, or green-black in summer when tornadoes crack the sudden stillness—strenuous spirochetes boring into the earth.

Up and down then back up again go the eyes leering at this structure of man's, named for a man who knew too well the bitter joys this sometimes idol incarnates: Richard Halliburton—a plaque beneath tells us—an explorer and traveler, an aviator who died when his own craft crashed: "A modern-day Icarus—he flew too close to the sun."

I STOOD THERE at the tower's base, a student once again. Wide-eyed, trembling. *What am I doing here?* Three hours back in town and I had called no one, seen no one, done no other thing than dream that strange dream, then rise for a shower and a car ride. My destination had been Braden's house. "Pleasant Hill" we had wryly, optimistically named it once, that falling down bungalow on a lump in the terrain—named it one gloriously drunken night after some house in some hideously Southern book, by some grandly Southern author. I wondered if he remembered all that.

The streets in that section of town are largely a grid, even so, I managed to meander. A seven minute straight shot, two lefts and a right, had become a trip through the Square and a ramble through the lanes of the park—an avoidance trip at its finest: "Oh, here's that pond. Look!" "The bandshell—Was it Dave Brubeck we heard that night?" "The zoo!" "Let's see, here is where we spray-painted 'No I-40' when they planned to build the interstate there and bring Cassina's famous *shvarzers* right to Esther Meyerman's front door." *Cassina, Cassina, Cassina.* Then to my old college. The tower. *What am I doing here?*

What am I doing here? It's time to go.

Braden, I don't even want to see you. Braden, it's time to see you.
Something shifted. The streets were the same. At once, little had changed. I drove, as I had hundreds of times, to the house. Now it all seemed matter-of-fact—the anxiety was underneath or else I was on top of it—like riding a horse.

Not a card, not a call. I took a chance: Maybe he's home, maybe he's not. I took the chance. Looping around the median and back down the block, I drove to the house, pulling up to the curb and killing the engine. Another shift: The horse made its presence known. Deep breath. *Now or never.*
How about never?
Deeper breath.
I opened the door. Shoes to the asphalt. Slammed the door. Too loud. A light on behind the sheer curtains. Not a stir, not a move.

Legs like rubber bands beneath me, wobbly knees—as I walked up the little slope, they actually gave once. *Get a grip! This is ridiculous. What the hell is wrong with me?*

Two steps. "Skit, skit" went the shoes against the concrete. Deeper breath. Shaking, literally shaking. Eyes spy the round bell to the right. Hand extends—vibrating—*Touch the button.*
R-i-n-n-n-n-g.

I jumped.

I could hear the thump and thud of feet across the hardwood floors inside, then a rattle of the knob. It was turning. Heart pounding in my chest, in my ears. That blood rushing sound. Cold darts shooting down my legs. The door opened before me. Light spilled out, meeting the light from the porch lamp.

Our eyes met and my teeth dug sharply into my lower lip from behind. "Hello, Braden."

"My God! Andrew Jackson Taylor!"

"As I live and breathe."

"What are you doing here?"

"I've been asking myself that same thing, Mr. O'Brien." I drew a deep breath, held it. "Pahhhhh" went its exhale. "Well," I said after a moment, "Cassina Gambrel is missing."

It was the "open sesame." Braden pushed against the door and held it back with one hand. "Would you like to come in?"

My eyes looked around quickly: The sooty fireplace, different picture, new paint—claret colored, refinished wood trim, curtains on the doors, stuffed chairs, brass lamps. Up to the light fixture—cleaned, polished. "No babies."

"What?"

He was looking at me with a puzzled expression and my eyes went back to the light. "No babies," I repeated and looked at him again.

"Oh." He snort-chuckled. "No. No babies. Long gone."

"Too bad ... " I said turning around to survey the full room. It had come a long way. Posh now. " ... You might have had something here, otherwise."

Braden laughed.

I held my arms wide open, "What happened?"

"Reconstruction."

Now I snorted. "It looks great."

"Thanks," he said. "Wanta' see the rest of it?"

"Sure."

There were no major structural changes that I could see, but the house looked completely transformed. Gone were the plaster chips, the gaping holes, the creaking floors. The walls were smooth, crisply painted in a palette of exquisite shades. New tile in the bathroom. Modern appliances in the kitchen. "All mod cons," Braden announced.

My old bedroom was now a den that Braden explained could double as a spare bedroom with its sleeper sofa.

I smelled money—fragrant and new.

"My God, Braden, I wouldn't have imagined it," I said. "Sorry, I don't mean ... "

"I know," he agreed, laughing.

"Surely, Mr.... what's his name?"

"Who?"

"The landlord— "

"Sevier."

"Sevier, that's it. Surely, he didn't do all this."

"Not a chance. He let me paint—no deduction on the rent, mind you—about a year after you left," Braden explained. "Then, I started doing a little bit more here and there and he took notice."

"Yeah ...?" I said.

"Saw that I was interested, decided to sell."

"You own it?"

"You betcha'."

"My God ... who'd have thought." My hand did a Jack Benny to my cheek and I stood there shaking my head. "Mmh!" I said, interrupting my own reverie. "And Sevier?"

"*Muerto.*"

I crossed myself.

"Say, here's something I recognize!" I exclaimed walking to the little service porch that now housed a washer and dryer.

"Oh, yes!" said Braden.

I looked at the milk crates that once held my book collection, now containing laundry supplies and assorted odds and ends.

"Want 'em back?" he offered.

"No, but the store whose loading dock they came from may! Whady'a reckon the statute of limitations is?"

" 'Bout ten years," he said dryly.

"Think I'm safe?"

"I think you are."

"I think I am, too." I looked at Braden. Wanted very much to hug him. Instead, I said, "Upstairs?"

"Still an apartment."

"Student?"

"Not on your life!"

We both laughed.

"She's a nurse at the medical center," he explained. "Quiet, thank God. Rent's paid on time. We rarely see each other."

"Well, some things change very little at least," I said. "You know: 'The mysterious tenant upstairs.' "

We both laughed nervously. Ha-ha-ha.

"Braden, I'm sorry." I heard myself blurting out. "Whatever it was, I'm sorry."

He waved the air with his left hand, dismissing it. "Forget it."

"Whew!" I exhaled. Then, "Cassina ... "

"Missing."

"Yes."

"Where?"

"No one knows."

"Dumb. Sorry."

He waved again.

"How long?"

"At least a week, ten days," he said. "The police aren't completely sure. Her car is gone, too. I forgot to tell you."

I thought of our phone call two days before and started to say something.

Apparently, Braden read my mind because he stopped me with an upheld palm, "Don't."

I had not given Braden any advance notice of my visit and he had the great grace not to mention it. He did, however, glance at his watch.

"I'm keeping you."

"No, really," he said. "Not at all."

"Sure?"

"Yes," he said with some degree of insistence. "Yes!" he added, as if to assure me.

"Okay!"

"Hungry?"

I had had nothing substantial since leaving Boston that afternoon. "Starved," I said.

"In or out?" he asked.

"Well, while I'm here, I should take advantage of Memphis' great food."

Braden just looked at me.

"In, please," I said sheepishly.

"In it is," he announced.

"If it's not too much trouble."

"Not at all," he said, leading the way to the kitchen.

"Tanks."

"Shoo-ah." He opened the refrigerator, began rummaging around, checking the bins. "Spaghetti?"

"Do you still make it as bad as you did?"

"Worse."

"Good, you're on. How can I help?"

"Well," he said, retrieving an onion, "how 'bout finding a pot to boil the pasta in."

"And where would that be?"

"Andrew Jackson," he said, adopting a speechifying attitude, "look to the kitchen cabinet." He pointed with a grand flourish.

Nervous Banter 101:

"Ah-ha-ha-ha," I replied in inscrutable Charlie Chan fashion, "so, Victor Braden O'Brien—if that is your real name!—we've come to that: Obscure historical puns on my name. You're out of your league—fair warning." I started to plunder through the pots and pans in the cabinet, clanging and banging, until I found an eight-quarter. "Ah-ha!"

Braden was already chopping away. "Yeah-yeah."

"Look what I found!"

"*Mazel-tov.*"

"And," I said brandishing the aluminum vessel, "to the Victor (yuk! yuk!) go the spoils!"

"Mmm," he grunted. "A true Jacksonianism. You know that thing you said a minute ago—about me being out of my league?"

"Y-e-e-e-s?"

"No, I'm not," he said with a simultaneous bite of his tongue and a sneer.

"Well!" I mustered all the haughtiness I could. I filled the pot and placed it on the stove, then turned to face Braden thrusting a bottle of wine and a corkscrew at me. "Cheers!"

"Up yours!"

"YOU KNOW WHAT I just thought of?" asked Braden as he tore a bunch of arugula into a teakwood bowl.

"What's that?"

"That first time I actually met Cassina," he said.

"Oh, God! That was—what—where?"

"Catering!"

"It was?" My memory was fuzzy.

"Yes, yes!" he said with excitement. "For the wedding of Edward Meyerman's daughter!"

"Oh, yes! Now I remember!"

"It was our senior year."

"No couldn't have been."

"Why not?" He finished preparing the salad and took it to the dining room table.

"Because," I said, following him into the room with the bread, "you met her before we went to the Horse Show and that had to be the year before we graduated."

"Are you sure?" Braden motioned me to take a seat, then said, "Light those candles, would you?"

I fumbled in my pocket for matches. "Of course, I'm sure! We graduated the first week of June and," I said, striking a match, then touching it to the wicks as I spoke, "everybody who is anybody knows the Charity

Horse Show is always the second week in June."
"Whoo!" and out went the match. I pulled my chair up to the table then patted the spot next to my glass. "You may lay your keys to Society right here, thank you."

"Right, right. Well ... " Braden raised his glass. "Here's to bad breeding."

"To bad breeding," I concurred with a clink.

"And," he added suddenly, "Welcome home."

A little snigger of a laugh escaped from me—the horse?—followed closely by a most gallant bow of my head. It was rapidly seeming that way again—home. As comfortable and familiar as all that. The repartee, the scenery, the company. Braden, himself, looked the same. Oh, sure, older, but the essence remained. Lanky, tall, the shock of brown curls—thinned a bit at the temples, whose wasn't?—the hands, except for their size, almost feminine in their gracefulness, dexterous fingers kneading when he spoke as if checking the very texture of the air.

"Yes, our junior year at Southwestern." He continued with the story.

"Right. Spring—April, I think."

"I think you're right," he said.

"Yes, I was surprised to hear from Cassina."

I HAD BEEN, too. Following that day in the bank's cafeteria, we had not communicated except for a card exchanged at Christmas.

"How'd ya like to make a fast fifty bucks?" the voice over the telephone asked.

" 'xcuse me, ma'am?" I said sleepily.

"A guy like you could use some walkin'-aroun' money, couldn't ya'?"

"Cassina!"

"*C'est moi!*"

"How are you?" I woke up fast for a Saturday morning.

" 'sgood as I ever was," came her answer.

"Well, Lord!" I said. "Then you're helpless."

Cassina's familiar cackle was like music over the wire.

"Listen," said Cassina. "Mr. Meyerman's eldest daughter, Chava-Sue ... "

"No!"

"Yes!" she continued, "Chava-Sue's gettin' herself hitched tomorrow at the Anashi' Susah ... "

"The what?"

"It's they synagogue, mule!"

"Oh ... You sure?"

"Close enough."

"Hmm."

"And it's gonna' be a big affair—a wing-ding."

"Naturally."

"Naturally," she repeated, "and since it's right there in your neighborhood 'n' all, I thought of you."

"For what?"

"Oh! Oh! Oh! I forgot." She started to laugh. "I was leavin' out the best part."

"Ye-e-e-e-s ... ?"

"We're short-handed. Need some extra help in the kitchen tomorrow morning."

"Cassina, I don't know anything about cooking," I started to protest.

"Bah! There's nothin' to it. It's *schleppin'*, 'n' slicin', 'n' choppin' mostly that we need you for. I'll show you everythin'."

"What time?" I asked.

"Eight o'clock."

"Yikes!"

"Fifty dollars cash—you'll be home by eight o'clock at night."

"Well, I could use the money ... "

"Of course you could," she agreed.

"Okay."

"Wonderful!" She seemed genuinely thrilled. "And bring that roommate of yours, Brandon ... "

"SHE ASKED FOR you specifically, too," I said to Braden.

"Braden."

"Whatever."

"Okay. But Cassina, it's all kosher, isn't it?"

"Yes ... "

"What do I know about kosher?"

"Dummy," she said. "It's easy. Just keep your *fleyshik* out of your *milchik*!"

"Huh?"

"See you tomorrow." She hung up.

"I WAS NEVER more tired in my life," said Braden.

"Me either," I agreed, shaking my head. "But it was fun. C'mon, admit it."

"Fun!" Braden protested. "Fun! You call being up to your ... your ... "

"*Shibboleth?*" I offered.

"Ha! Whatever! ... in chicken liver 'fun'?"

"You loved it."

"Oh, please!" he said. "There ... there ... there we were, exhausted already by eleven o'clock in the morning and that caterer wanted four-hundred-fifty plates of chopped liver globs on lettuce."

"Cassina showed you how, didn't she?"

"Did she ever!" Braden proffered the wine bottle.

"Lay on, MacDuff."

He poured himself another glass, too, and continued his story. "Whatever happened to spoons is what I wanted to know."

"You had on gloves," I explained plainly. "Opera length, too, as I recall. Very fashionable."

He let me get away with that last. "Plastic gloves do not keep out the *feel*, the horrible, gunky, indescribable *feel* of chicken liver, eggs, and onions clinging to your hands and arms."

"How else you gonna mix 'em in those quantities, Victor Braden O'Brien?" I was taking Cassina's role now.

"Or the sound," he continued, ignoring me, "not unlike the sound horse manure makes when you are running barefoot through a pasture in the springtime and stumble upon it."

"Vulgarity!" I accused.

"Absolutely!" he cried.

"She offered you olives ... "

" ... for my ears. Ha! Ha!" he said sarcastically.

I began to shake with laughter. "Well ... "

"And those olives!"

"Well, you do have a point there."

Braden's head shook in disgust. "Do you remember this, Jackson?"

"In stereo and technicolor."

He described the routine: "One salad plate, one curly lettuce leaf, one scoop of liver, one stuffed green olive—pimento side up—dead center on top."

"She was thrilled, Braden ... "

"She told me they looked like tits!"

"But very *nice* tits, Braden."

"All right, all right." He pointed his index finger at me and bore down on me with his eyes the way Cassina did. "But ... she went too far with the melon balls!"

"Agreed."

Braden stopped for a moment, then laughed before saying, "I remember how much I wanted to meet her after all your stories that first summer."

"She wanted to meet you, too," I said quietly. My hand toyed with the candle holder, turning the square pedestal around.

"That was a good summer," Braden said.

"So was the next."

We both looked at each other. Is "wistful" the right word? Do men get "wistful?" "Melancholy?" Better. Not quite. What's wrong with these words ...?

Braden was the first to speak. "So ... "

"*Nu*," I said.

He chuckled. "So ... "

"What's to be done?" I cupped my palm too close to the flame.

"Nothing," he said.

"Nothing?"

"We wait."

"The police ...?"

"Working as hard as they can apparently. Meyerman has called up his wisest cronies, pulled every available string."

"How's he taking it? Do you know?" I reached for my glass.

"Hard, so I hear. A client of mine who's also in the banking industry knows him real well."

"Who's that?"

"Oh, you wouldn't know her. Works for a big new bank that built headquarters Out East—commissioned two murals from me for the new lobby."

"Excellent," I said. I was genuinely impressed. The guy had moved up and ahead in the world. "Congratulations."

"Thanks."

"Anyway ... " *Enough of that.*

"Anyway," he continued, "she's known Meyerman a long time, came by the studio the other day and said that he's really broken up. Really worried."

"Any clues? Any suspicions?"

"Nothing. No evidence of foul-play except the missing car and the missing her."

I felt frustrated. Told him so.

"Of course you are. We all are," he responded.

"I want to do something."

"Such as ...?"

"Talk to people. Ask around. Anything."

"Have at it, Jackson. The police have probably covered most of the obvious territory by now."

"Well, I'm here."

"And I'm glad," he said.

It took me only a half a moment before I agreed. "So am I."

"How long are you here?" He picked up a plate.

"I'll help you with those." We began to clear the dishes as I answered his question. "I begged a week. Ten days really. I have to be back in class a week from Monday."

"That's a good amount of time. Let's hope we know something before then."

"I hope so. I'm so frustrated."

Braden said, "You're in good company there, old boy."

"There's a comfort."

"Where ya staying?" he asked.

"The hotel across from the library."

"Comfortable?"

"Fine, I guess."

"You're welcome to stay here, Jackson."

"Oh, well that's good of you. I think ... uh ... I'm fine where I am."

Braden blew out a candle. "Okay."

"Thanks for the offer, though."

"Sure," he said. We both started at the sound of a key in the door.

Turning towards the front door just as it opened, I saw a familiar face.

Braden leaned over the table and extinguished the remaining candle with one short breath.

Chapter Seven

"A FROG HE WENT A COURTIN' AND HE DID RIDE"

LAURA FRANKLIN STOOD in the doorway of "Pleasant Hill" looking like the sun, the moon, and the stars. Oh, yeah—all of that. Her hair cascaded—that is the only word for it—cascaded down to her shoulders in splashes of amber. I drew a deep breath. She noticed me there in the archway between the dining room and the living room and for a moment, her eyes dropped and a finger twirled lazily in a wave of hair as if she were a girl again. She raised her silvery blue eyes slowly until they met mine and I knew at once she was not. No. At one glance, it was evident that Laura Franklin had matured into the very epitome of a fine, handsome Southern woman.

I stepped forward as she did, her hand extending slowly, then her left reached up to clutch me around my shoulder. She fixed me firmly in her gaze and spoke my name as if it were a commandment, "Jackson Taylor."

"Laura."

"My goodness. It is you."

"Hello, Laura," I said.

Her hand clutched more tightly against my shoulder, then she was kissing my cheek. "As she did, I breathed in the fragrance from her. She still smelled of honeysuckle as I remembered.

"I had a feeling you'd come," she said. "Didn't I, Braden?"

I turned to see him standing there against the arch, darkness behind him, where a moment ago I had been. Then it hit me and it was my turn to fix a gaze.

He noticed it I know, because something small changed then around the line of his cheek just beside the nostrils.

My lips now arranged themselves in a forced smile so tight I felt my eyes crinkle.

She broke from me then and went to his side. "Hello, darling." She kissed his cheek as his arm encircled her.

"Hello, there," he said to her. "All the while, he kept his eyes on mine.

I did not move from the place I stood, only raised my chin slightly and said, "Laura Franklin, how good it is to see you."

If I am to tell you anything of Laura Franklin, I must first speak to you of Biffy Lee Pettigru.

"SO," SAID CASSINA, "you're invited to the Horse Show?"

"Yes, I am. Isn't that too much?"

"Who you going with?" she wanted to know. Something in her tone indicated that she held a genuine concern about this, although she did her best to feign indifference. *Could it be that she was looking out for my social well-being?*, I wondered.

"Well, Cassina, I'm going with Laura Franklin. Her parents have a box and there's room for tonight, so Laura asked me."

Laura Franklin was a secretary in the mortgage loan department at the bank. She had graduated college the week before, so you can figure for yourself that she was a year older than me. I wondered if Cassina would comment on my continued trend in "older women."

"Well," said Cassina, "Laura Franklin. Why, I think that's fine, jus' fine." She grinned broadly; I was surprised. Surprised, too, at my relief that Cassina seemed to approve.

"Laura's a lovely girl, jus' lovely," said Cassina.

"Well, yes. Yes, I suppose she is, Cassina," I said.

"Tell me, how'd you two meet?"

I wasn't sure that I trusted this part of Cassina—she was oozing a little too much charm, if you know what I mean. "Ummm ... " I began hesitantly, "let's see. We met at work, of course. She's a secretary ... "

"Yes, I know," Cassina said, apparently eager for more delicious details.

"Of course you know," I said. "You know everything about everybody."

She looked me dead in the eye and said with complete earnestness, "Well, not everybody."

"Ha!" I scoffed at her. "When the CIA's in trouble, I bet they come to you!"

Cassina said nothing, just turned her head to one side, smiled that half-smile of hers, and dropped her eyes in mock-bashfulness.

"You're a nut."

"It's true, I know," she vowed. "But," she said impatiently, "you still haven't told me what I want to know."

"There's nothing to tell! She's a secretary. We met at the office during the normal course of things, said 'hi' a few times, got to talking, had coffee in the lunch room and she asked me out." Why was I blushing?

"Coffee!" Cassina said the word as if it meant "intercourse." "Coffee?" she repeated.

"Yes, coffee." My irritation on the rise—"*Coffee.*"

"Oh, my," said Cassina, "I didn't know it had come to this! *Coffee!*" she said again.

"Stop saying that word!" I demanded. "You make it sound so dirty."

"Dirty? Why," (hand flying to breast) "I don't think it's *dirty*. If two people over the age of consent ... " she gave me a quick once-over, " ... and I realize they have lowered that age since my time ... but if two people want to have coffee together and they both agree to it, I see nothing wrong with it. Certainly nothing 'dirty,' if that's even the right word!"

I was ready to strangle her. "Stop it, Cassina!"

"Well, all right. If you insist." All innocence now—"I was just interested, that's all."

This time I caught her turning her lips inward, trying to suppress a laugh.

"What is all this?". I was petulant again, knew it, knew too that if I stayed that way, I could abandon all hope.

"I'm just trying to prepare you."

"Prepare me for what?"

"The Horse Show, of course," she said, as if I were a complete idiot.

"What's to prepare for? It's a Horse Show. It should be fun," I said.

"Oh, it is. It is. A lot of fun. It's quite a big deal, too. Everybody's there. A lot of fun," she repeated. Cassina looked at me. "You've never been have you?"

"No."

"Oh, don't worry, it'll be fine."

There was just enough a hint of foreboding in her voice to make me ask, "What's to worry?"

"Nothing!" Her voice rose about an octave when she said that. "Nothing at all," she said, making a distinctive wave with her hand. "It's really wonderful. Really." Cassina looked at me again. I was unconvinced. "You'll love it." As usual, had she stopped there, things would be different. But of course, she wouldn't or couldn't. "Especially the steeplechase. That's the best part."

"How come?"

"You'll see. All I can say is the smart money says she will."

"Whoa! What? Wait a minute, Cassina, I'm lost." 'Deed I was, too. "She, who? Will, what?"

"She—Biffy Lee Pettigru. Will—fall off her horse."

"What?" I laughed so hard the chair shook.

Cassina lowered her voice and darted her eyes around quickly. Another conspiracy. "Every year, there is an unofficial pool that bets on whether or not Biffy Lee Pettigru will fall off her horse in the steeplechase."

"No!" I was shocked.

Cassina's right hand flew up. I covered my mouth, giggling.

Cassina looked around again. "Biffy Pettigru couldn't ride a horse for Come-to-Jesus."

I wasn't exactly sure what that meant, but I got the general idea.

"And," Cassina continued, "if she's doin' poorly in the steeplechase (and believe you me, she usually is), she'll fall off her horse before she finishes."

"No!"

"She started it years ago as a face-saving measure. That way, she can always blame the horse, claim it threw her—too wild or too skittish—don't matter. It happened a few times. Then, pretty soon, people caught on and began to watch for it. It's practically an event unto itself."

"Why doesn't she just give up riding?" I really was green.

Cassina fixed me with another look. "And give up all that prestige? Don't you be lookin' too hard for any logic in this, Jackson Taylor."

Suddenly, panic struck. "I can't go!" There I would be, primed for an outrageous spectacle, on my first date with Laura Franklin, with her parents in her parent's box for all the world (or at least part of mine) to see. "I can't go!" I said again. "I'll never be able to keep a straight face!"

"*Pish!*" said Cassina Gambrel, "You'll love it."

I HAD PICKED up Laura in my green Toyota at her parent's house near Memphis State University. Following a nice supper out, we made our way east to Germantown which still had a pleasant suburban feel to it despite the phenomenal growth it was undergoing. In 1970, its population had been about 3700 souls scattered across a village and several horse farms. By the time I first saw it, it had more than tripled its size and nowadays is a nearly unrecognizable shadow of its former self at right around 36,000 inhabitants. It was pretty; the schools were good; it was predominately populated by white people; and it was growing increasingly expensive as a separately incorporated entity from the city of Memphis with its taxes and school busing, and which, somewhat like a ravenous amoeba unable to stop itself, was busily gobbling up the country-side all around through rapid annexation.

Germantown was fighting valiantly to retain its country and "more horses per capita than anywhere" ambiance. Along the shoulders of the main thoroughfares, there were still signs posted declaring "Speed Limit 40, Horses 10."

Laura directed my way through the old town with its one-building city hall/firehouse/police station adjacent to the railroad tracks that ran smack through its center.

"It's wonderful," I said as we passed a row of old churches, one it seemed, for each Protestant denomination—with the Methodists in brick and the Baptists in white clapboard. The town seemed to be a microcosm of Western Tennessee charm. We turned and passed the old water tower, then approached the sprawling high school complex which stood in stark contrast to the old-town character of the place.

"They keep building," Laura explained, "trying to keep up with the students that keep pouring into the place: Folks fleeing Memphis, out-of-towners looking for what they perceive as a safe refuge."

Traffic was overwhelming, jamming the tiny streets. We sat for a while at a standstill looking down the road to the place ahead where cars turned in front of a brick building.

"What's that?" I asked her.

"The new library. The grounds are just behind it."

"Laura, I had no idea this was such a big event."

"Oh, yes," she said, "everybody has to come for at least one night. Especially the newcomers trying so eagerly to fit in."

"But what about you? You don't live anywhere near here," I said, "but your folks have a box."

"Of course!" She gave me a little rap on the arm.

I looked at her quizzically and she tossed her head back with a laugh. As she did, the light from the setting sun struck those tresses and all my hot Southern blood fairly bubbled. She was, without a doubt, the loveliest creature I had ever seen.

"I guess it's business; I know it's social," she was saying, but I was busy studying her exquisitely colored eyes. She stopped suddenly and turned her head away slightly, surveying the field outside her window. "Is there something wrong?"

"No, not wrong," I said tenderly. The color filled in her cheeks. "You do look mighty pretty sittin' there." And indeed she did. She was dressed in a simple sun dress—I remember it like it was yesterday—yellow with brown accents and tiny white flowers—something small and delicate—daisies, I believe. Yes! daisies they were—like miniature fireworks bursting.

"Thank you, Jackson," she said, lowering her eyes in her fashion. As she raised them, she turned to look me full in the face. "You look fine, too."

And I thought I had died on the spot.

When my voice came back to me, I said, "Oh, thanks. I wasn't sure. Cassina said ... "

"Cassina!" Laura laughed.

Why did I mention Cassina?! "Yes ... "

"Oh, that's right. You drive her, don't you?"

"Well, only sometimes this summer—not like last. It's a paying job now, you know."

"Oh, yes," she said.

"So, it's only on occasion that I take her around now. I think somebody else does otherwise." Actually, I knew that to be true, but for some reason, I wanted to distance myself from Cassina now, perhaps to impress my date that my job involved much more than chauffeuring around Cassina Gambrel.

"She's so funny," Laura said and I relaxed a bit. "But, you know," she said with a hint of warning, "she's thick as thieves with Mr. Meyerman."

"Oh, that's all right. We get along just great."

"So I gather," Laura said.

Traffic began to move and I shifted my foot from the brake to the gas. "What do you mean?"

"You're back, aren't you?"

"Yes, I am. And it looks like if things go well, I'll have an offer to stay on part-time in the fall when school starts up," I said with pride.

"That's great," said Laura.

"Thanks ... " She smiled a smile that just about stopped my heart. I couldn't imagine that I should be so lucky as to be with this girl—the result being that nervous chatter thing I do—avoiding the moment at hand. "Uh ... anyway, Cassina indicated that maybe it was a little highfalutin out here."

She laughed again. "You look terrific." She ran her fingertips down my lapel. "I love your blazer."

The car ahead of me had slowed and as I was beaming at Laura, I almost rear-ended it. My foot slammed the brake and we jolted forward.

"Sorry," I said, looking up at her; but mercifully, Laura had turned away again and was busily rolling down the window.

"Listen," she said ecstatically, "I hear the music!"

THE ARENA WAS thick with people: Men in cowboy hats escorted women in pearls; ladies in designer jeans and silk blouses clung to the arms of gentlemen in ultrasuade and khakis. From painted wooden stalls, vendors hawked red wine and pork barbecue sandwiches, beer and corn-on-the-cob. All the boxes (where Laura and I sat with her parents) were taken. Packed. Across from us at ten o'clock—Edward Meyerman and friends. Curiously absent from his side was Mrs. Meyerman. He saw Laura and I together, smiled and nodded our way. This thrilled me no end. The boss had noticed! We grinned and nodded respectfully in return. The general admission area, too, was at capacity, while hundreds more stood around the edges. The general mood was gay and as spirited as the horses trotting in the ring under the white lights which beat down upon them. Despite the warm weather, a band—remnants from the high school, I presumed—stood playing in full uniform: Red jackets, white trousers, and hats repletely springing forth red and white plumes.

"They're really good," I said, leaning over to speak in Laura's ear.

"Yes, they are," she said.

The band started "When the Saints Go Marching In." Hands began clapping in time. Mine clapped right along.

Mrs. Franklin leaned over in my direction, "Jackson?"

"Yes, ma'am?"

"Jackson, are you enjoying yourself?"

"This is great!" I shouted over the band. "I had no idea that anything like this existed."

Mrs. Franklin twittered. "Oh my, yes, honey. And the best is yet to come."

"There's more?"

"Lord, yes! 'xcuse me." She leaned the other way. "What dear? ... Oh, yes, of course." Now back to me. "Jackson, Mr. Franklin wants to know if you care for any more wine."

"Oh, no, thank you. I'm fine."

She grinned and cooed. As she turned her head back to her husband, the wind must have been blowing correctly because I could hear her say, "See dear, I told you."

Laura's elbow dug into my side.

In the arena, four men busily worked to set up for the next event.

"I really didn't know I would have this much fun," I said to Laura.

"Well, I'm glad you are," she said. Laura slipped her left hand through the crook in my arm and scooted in a bit.

Perfect, I thought. *This is just absolutely one hundred percent perfect.*

"Ladies and gentlemen," a man's voice boomed over a loud speaker, "please welcome the pride of Tennessee—the Walkers!"

"Bring 'em on!" I said enthusiastically. Laura moved closer.

The band began "The Tennessee Waltz" as the horses came high-stepping out. Applause swept through the arena; the crowd rose to its feet.

"Dixie!" I sighed. "Ah'm in Dixie!"

"Stop it!" she teased as she snuggled nearer to me.

"Oh, Laura, this is the life! The horses, the food, the fresh air, the music!"

"The people ... " she chimed in.

"Well, maybe ... "

"Jackson!" she protested.

"Okay, the people." We laughed. "Thank you so much for inviting me."

"Well, Jackson," she sounded surprised, "I'm sure glad you're having such a good time."

"Oh, I am. Who could ask for more?"

Some fallen angel must have heard me, because, looking back on it now, I can practically hear a clap of thunder and see the lightning bolt in the sky as I recall those words.

"Dear ... " It was Mrs. Franklin.

Laura smiled broadly. "Well, hello."

My eyes went from looking at her mouth to the one she directed her words to. I didn't move a muscle, but simply stared. In front of us stood the most ... mmm, how shall I say this? ... "horsey" woman I have ever seen. Black velvet riding hat over a l-o-o-o-n-g face featuring two wide-set eyes the color of chestnuts. Black velvet jacket straining ever so hard to close in front over the white blouse and jabot. The camel-colored jodhpurs only emphasized the creature's ample hip room. And of course there were the requisite black leather boots on the feet which were spread approximately two-and-a-half feet apart. My lips froze in a pucker. My eyes continued their saucer-shaped stare. *Please, God, no!*

She whipped her riding crop through the air a few times as she spoke to Laura. "Whip" "Whip" "Whip" she punctuated.

No, no, no, no, no, no.

"Jackson," Laura said.

No, please, please, please...

"Jackson, I'd like to introduce you to someone."

There is no way out of here is there? None. None at all. I am trapped. Trapped! Trapped, I say!

My body cranked around mechanically. I heard Laura's voice in progress, " ... may I present Jackson Taylor. Jackson, this is Biffy Lee Pettigru."

Biffy Lee's gums parted. "Hello!" she whinnied.

My mouth opened and closed like a ventriloquist's dummy. "How do you do?"

"Laura tells me you work at the bank with her." ("Whip" "Whip")

"Why, yes. That is correct." *And I've heard so much about you! ... Don't say it!* I did.

"You have?" ("Pat, pat, pat" went the crop in her palm.)

"Uh . . . yes . . . uh . . . didn't . . . I . . . uh . . . read something-about-you-in-the-paper-the-other-day-in-connection-with-the-Show?" I hadn't.

"Why, yes!" ("Whip-whip-whip!" "Whip-whip-whip-whip-whip!") "How nice of you to have noticed!" ("Whip-whip")

Safe!

"Jackson's very attentive," said Laura, giving a tug at my arm.

"Oh, I just bet he is, Laura!" ("Slice, whoosh!")

I jumped. *Fine, I'm fine, I'm fine. Do not, Biffy Lee—whatever you do—do not flair your nostrils or you're dog chow!*

"Will you be riding tonight, Mrs. Pettigru?"

"Well, yes, Laura," Biffy Lee said sportily, "you know I am!"

"Oh, good luck, Mrs. Pettigru. Be careful."

"Thank you, dear."

Laura nudged me.

"Yes," I said, "good luck. And so nice to meet you." *Don't push it.*

Biffy Lee grinned from ear to ear, which was quite a long ways. "Nice to meet you, too, Mr. Taylor." She knighted me with her crop. Then she gave Laura a knowing woman-to-woman look and said, "Cheerio!"

"Cheerioats ... uh ... oh! Cheerio!" I waved after her. *Damn, almost!*

Laura and I sat down again.

"Jackson, is something —"

"No!" Perhaps my response was a trifle quick.

Laura studied my face.

"Fine, fine, fine," I said with three accompanying pats on the back of her hand à la Biffy Lee.

"Are you sure —"

"Fine, fine, fine!" I repeated.

We sat there for a few moments watching the Walking Horses.

"She's an old friend of the family," Laura explained.

You hate me, don't you, God?
"Mother and her go way back. Before college, even."
Of course they do. "That's nice." Scanning the grounds, I tried for anything to change the subject. "Oh, my, look there," I said as a horse lifted its tail.

THE ARENA HAD been expertly set up and so had I. Hurdles of various heights camouflaged by potted shrubs lined the course. My palms sweated.

The announcer had called everyone's attention to "Tonight's Premiere Event." I accepted Mr. Franklin's previous offer of another drink. Then another. Meanwhile, a rider had executed the course perfectly; the band played "Stairway to Paradise." "They know everything, don't they?" I asked Laura whose face was beginning to look ashen.

"Are you okay?" she asked me after the second rider finished.

"Oh, sure!" *God, these lights are hot!* I smiled at her and crinkled my nose.

Over at the ten o'clock spot, there was movement in the Meyerman box: Men standing, ladies rearranging their feet. Waves and handshakes.

"What's she doing here?" I groaned.

"Who, Jackson?" Laura implored.

I nodded towards the Meyerman box.

Cassina was dressed in what can best be described as "Mint-Julep Renaissance." It was silk, I think, but whatever it was, there was lots of it. Yards and yards. Aqua and turquoise roses on a lime green background. The boldness of the pattern was broken only by the severity of the plunging neckline. Her breasts looked like two hams peeking from behind the drapes. It was a very ... uh ... *shiny* outfit dimmed but slightly by the sheer organza overlaying the skirt which directed the eye—"commanded" would be a better word—toward the double row of ruffles at the hemline. She was crowned with a wide floppy hat crafted from the same material as the dress and she clutched a little white handkerchief in the delicate club of her hand. I had an uncanny urge to sing "The Wreck of the Edmund Fitzgerald."

Cassina caught my eye and delivered her best back-handed Windsor wave.

"She always comes to the Horse Show, Jackson. What's wrong? I thought she was your friend."

"I thought so, too."

"Ladies and gentlemen, our next competitor, Mrs. Plunkett Pettigru."

Warm applause from the audience.

"Plunkett?"

"Uncle Plunk," Laura explained. "Jackson, you look so pale."

Horse and rider circled the arena almost as one.

T-rot, t-rot, t-rot. Up! Applause.

T-rot, t-rot, t-rot, t-rot. Up! Applause.

I glanced at Laura who was smiling sweetly. I returned the smile, again with the icky crinkly nose. *For God's sake, stop doing that!*

T-rot, t-rot, t-rot, t-rot.

T-rot, t-rot, t-rot, t-rot.

Did I dare? Oh, yes. My eyes, doubtless possessed by Satan, himself, riveted towards Cassina. The lacy hankie still dangled from her hand which was poised at the corner of her mouth. Her face, beatific as an angel. *She's got a thousand on this, minimum.*

Applause.

The horse circled the arena, gaining momentum. Ahead, a hurdle: Four horizontal poles, high as a country fence. A noticeable rise in the chests of the audience. I had to look.

T-rot, t-rot, t-rot.

T-rot, t-rot, t-rot.

Then, as if trained, the horse stopped a full one yard short of the jump. Biffy Lee executed a little quiver coupled with a brief look of surprise, then slid counter-clockwise halfway around her horse—still gripping with thighs that must have been capable of cracking walnuts—and finally fell—oof!—onto the sawdust.

"Hoh!" aspirated the audience.

Silence fell like mankind after the apple.

Except for one: One tiny, insignificant speck of humanity in one tiny, insignificant box in one tiny stadium. It started someplace deep, low down, *way* down—the toes, perhaps. A titter, it might be called. Then a snort. Then a chuckle on top of a tee-hee, followed by a belly-shake and a guffaw. "Ha-ha-ha-ha!" The screams poured from me like shit from a goose until my whole body shook.

Biffy Lee stood up, dusted sawdust from her jodhpurs, and began to limp from the arena. I shrieked. She shot me a look that could have killed a water-buffalo. I doubled-over clutching my sides. The audience covered Biffy Lee's exit with polite applause while the band quickly launched into an appropriate selection—"Louie, Louie" I believe it was.

With the music, the crowd began chattering while I choked and coughed. Laura delivered a karate chop of no small force between my shoulder blades, as I looked through tear-soaked eyes to see Cassina Gambrel, face buried in her white gloves.

Chapter Eight

*"To A Boon Southern Country
He Is Fled,
And Now In Happier Air"*
—**Matthew Arnold**
"Thyrsis"

ON THE SOUTH side of campus, amidst the massive oaks and poplars studding the earth between the horseshoe drive known as Library Lane and the busy thoroughfare that is the North Parkway, lies a little garden that in late spring and summer is the fairest place on earth. Driving past it in the warmer months from late March onward when its shrubs thicken and its old dogwoods explode in a riot of pink and white, one would not know, had one not been let in on the secret of its existence, that on the other side of what appears to be merely a high hedge, a charmed circle exists.

It is entered through a well-concealed break in the green on a path of fieldstone slabs placed every couple of feet—just far enough apart to make a journey to the garden following a storm a potentially mud-splattered affair. Once inside, you will find a grassy expanse encompassed by azaleas—coral, pink, white, when blooming—and on the far side, a flat cement stage elevated no more than two feet, on which commencement exercises are held the first week in June.

The garden is, amazingly enough, well-respected by students and outsiders alike who know of it. It would be easy for anyone with a taste for destruction to access it and do real damage. Perhaps my telling you about it is not such a good thing after all. I hope that your knowledge will also breed respect and should you ever find yourself there, please treat it kindly.

IT WAS ON that bare stage in late July of 1979, that Laura Franklin and I found ourselves.

"What do you call them?" Before I could answer her, she went on, "You know, I went to school here for four years and never once did I learn the true names of these." Her hand was gliding across the smooth surface of a small sculpture at the base of the stage. "Neriads?"

"No."

"Something like that ... Gargoyles are on gutters, aren't they?"

"Sally sells salamanders instead of salads."

"Stop it!"

"Nymphs."

"More than that."

"Don't know."

"Yes, you do."

"Sorry, can't help."

"Why are you being so obstinate?"

I folded my arms across my chest. "Who's obstinate?"

"You are! You, you, you!" She raised her arms, silly now, in imitation of Frankenstein's monster. "I must 'keel' you now," she growled in her best Indeterminate-European accent.

"Wait, look!" I turned away from her and raised my own arms. The white spill of light from the street lamp across the Lane cast our shadows over the stage where we sat. I formed a swan and moved its "beak" in time as I sang:

> "I come from the deep
> from the land of the nymphs
> and other mysterious creatures—
> I'm not a gargoyle
> or such as that,
> because I got better features."

"You're making this up ... " She gave me a push.
"Damn right I am."
I continued improvising:

> "I gots two arms
> and a tail like a fish.
> With that I can make do—
> I don't need a horse
> 'cause I'm a real dish,
> not like Mrs. Pettigru-oo."

"Jackson!"

> "If I had six legs,
> I'd be like her—"

"Stop it!"

> "But as-of-now
> I'm a perfect triad,
> For the mythical creature
> I am, my dear,
> is no other thing
> than a ... naiad."

"Naiad," she sighed, "that's it." She snuggled behind me with her head on my shoulder and her arms around my waist.

> "And I am in love,
> in love, you see
> with a girl
> who's here in the grass.
> And I love her most—
> whoopee! whoopee!—
> 'cause she loves me
> even when I've been an ass."

"Your meter's off."
"Does it matter?" I asked.
Her response was to kiss me. Our bodies shifted toward each other and we embraced more passionately still.

The cement stage must have been terribly hard and uncomfortable for both of us. Is it being twenty-one that makes those things bearable or unimportant?

"Do you mean that, Jackson?" she asked.
"What's that?"
"That part about loving a girl."
"I'm afraid so. Didn't intend to."
"Well now," was all she said.

I gazed into those eyes of hers and all the world vanished save her and me. It's true.

"I've been meaning to tell you for the longest time," I said.

"When did you first know?"

"Mmm ... " I thought back, "when I was so angry after the Horse Show."

"Angry?"

"At the world; at everything; at Cassina for setting me up like that."

Laura grimaced, "Come on."

"Well, her sense of humor has been known to border on the epic."

I HAD MADE a full confession to Laura the next day in person after pleading with her to meet me at a neutral spot—the band shell—to talk. She had allowed me to drive her home that night, albeit in silence. After I had returned to my house—mine and Braden's—I had a heart-to-heart with him.

"Forget it," he counseled me. "It was just one of those stupid things. She," (he meant Biffy Lee) "sounds like a real piece of work to me."

"Oh, God," I had said (two or three times as I recall) sitting there in the shabby living room.

"Forget it," he repeated. "Nobody will remember it tomorrow."

"She will." (I meant Laura Franklin.)

"Uh-oh," said Braden.

"What?"

Braden made a noise like an airplane crashing.

"What?" I said again, this time with anger.

Braden's forehead wrinkled up. "Oh, blind, blind, blind," he said. He held his hand up in the air a few inches from my face. "Demons, come out. Be healed!"

"Will you stop that!" I slapped his hand good and hard to which he responded by laughing. "Damn you, Braden! What the hell is wrong with you?"

"I'm going to bed." He strode down the hall to his room with me close on his heels.

"No, you're not!" I insisted like a whiny child.

He laughed louder.

"Not until you tell me what's wrong!"

Braden paused at his door. "Well, old guy, let's just say it looks to me like Biffy Lee Pettigru isn't the only one who took a fall tonight."

"What do you mean?" I demanded.

"What do you mean?" he mimicked.

"Stop that, you asshole!"

Braden looked me straight in the eye. "Y'always did have a way with words, Jackson." He examined my shoulder, then pulled an imaginary fleck from my hair and touched it to his tongue. "Mmm. Sawdust. My favorite."

"Fuck you, Braden."

Braden minced and puckered. "You brute. You big bully." He turned and went inside his room. Before closing the door completely, he made a little air kiss with his lips and said, "Nighty-night ... Stud."

I stood there in the hall, metaphorical pants hovering around my knees. "Prick," I called.

"Horrors!" I heard through the door, followed by peals of laughter.

"Shitty little prick!"

"Ooh, flatterer," he said.

"Bastard!"

"Sticks and stones may break my bones ... "

I was talking to a door. And a brick wall.

Before calling Laura the next morning, I first rang up the home of one Cassina Gambrel.

"Just what in the hell were you doing there last night?" I shouted through the telephone.

Cassina's response was pure Faulkner, "My, my," she said, "a body does get around."

"Can it!"

She was silent.

"What are you trying to do to me, Cassina?"

"Bring you into the real world," she said. "There's a whole other you in there, just waitin' to get out." Her tone suddenly became formal as if someone had walked into the room. "And good morning to you, too, Mr. Taylor."

"Cassina Gambrel, there are days— "

She didn't let me finish. "It's a crap shot, Jackson. Y'pays yo'r money; y'takes yo'r chances."

"Meyerman ... "

"Not a problem. Jus' you leave him to me."

"Cassina ... !"

"Thank you for callin', Mr. Taylor, an' you have a happy day now, you hear?"

Click.

"JACKSON," SAID LAURA in the garden. "She's too much of an influence on you."

"Well—" I said, getting to my feet—"I have to stretch—" I explained. "—not anymore. Not now." My arms reached up. *Could I touch that sky?* I stood on my toes.

"What do you mean?" she asked from where she sat.

"It's you. You're the influence. Look ... " I pointed to a vine twining near a rhododendron at the edge of the stage. "Honeysuckle." I ambled over to it.

She was behind me. "Jackson .... " Her voice had a pleading quality to it. I did not turn around, but reached out to pluck a cluster from the vine. "When I was a kid in Knoxville, we used to drink the nectar from these."

"Jackson!"

"What is it, Laura?" I asked, turning to face her.

"I love you, too," she said. Simple as all that.

Is it an institution peculiar to the South? Romance, that is—love?—the Romantic notion that one could actually be "in love" in a matter of six weeks or less? Is it the sultry weather or the stars in a Tennessee sky or just the way a spray of honeysuckle looks in a young lady's hair? Or is it simply youth?

Chapter Nine

His Way

FROM THERE TO here seems a long way. Where the wrong turn happened remains unclear to me. The kind of moments in the garden which I have just described are the kind of moments that inexperienced men will store up to use as fuel for their next moves on their great quests to conquer the world. Laura Franklin being safe in my pocket was as sure a bet to me as Biffy Lee falling off her horse.

"In my pocket" is a phrase which some of you will rail against, perhaps justifiably. It is the type of phrase which seems to objectify her rather than acknowledge her as a full-fledged human being. And she was that—capable of anything and everything.

Having her "safe in my pocket" sounds, too, like ownership, and I am not at all certain, at this juncture, that one "has" love, that it is something one "owns". "Partakes of" might be more apt. "Gives" is the most mature component in that most complex of emotions, emotional transactions. "Gives" is the part that only recently have I come to understand, to acknowledge.

"Have" is the way I looked at it then. You see, it was a terrible misapprehension that I suffered under then:

That friends, careers, life, love and lovers were something that one chose from a menu B la carte: I'll start with two highly nuanced friendships, follow those with three or four wild adventures. Next, the sweetest kind of lover (whose depth of feeling I can not possibly return). Once sated with all of that, I'll consume the degree (*magna cum laude* with Phi Beta Kappa relish), then the career B la mode. Oh, I'm sorry, were we talking human lives here? Gluttony, thy name is ... You fill in the blank.

The ten months following, which included my senior year in college, became the busiest I have ever known. Certainly, though, the path for a career in banking—to which I believed myself to be thoroughly devoted—got well-paved. Connections were being made, responsibility demonstrated, and apparently, the admiration of my superiors was being earned.

One afternoon in November, Meyerman, himself, even had me to his office for tea—not quite the power gig that lunch would have been, but more appropriate: I was, after all, still an undergraduate and a part-time employee. An honor, this. A golden opportunity. His agenda, he stated, was to discuss my future. Mine, was to shut up and listen (little by little I was growing increasingly less green).

Meyerman saw a "bright future" for me within the industry, was I interested in continuing?

"Yes, sir, very much."

"Wonderful, wonderful."

I smiled.

He asked what I thought of the city.

"I've grown to be very fond of it: It's people, especially. There's a much more diverse community here than I realized initially. And I think there's a tremendous opportunity for development here."

"Yes?"

"Oh, yes." (Clear throat, sip tea.) "The revitalization of downtown is beginning—the restoration of the Peabody Hotel, stirrings on Cotton Row and Beale Street ... "

Meyerman nodded.

"And Out East, well actually further than that, the suburbs—it's amazing." *Best not to bring up my specific adventures in Germantown.* "It's like another city is growing out there."

Meyerman swallowed a bit of scone and reached for his knife. "I've seen it change a lot," he said. "Time was, ten years ago, we thought it all but lost. Downtown was dead. Assassinations. Riots. White flight."

"Mmh."

"You know something about all that, I believe."

"Yes, sir. I've done some reading, talked to some people ... "

"And you were here the summer before last. I believe that's when you first joined us here." Meyerman buttered a piece of scone. (It was clear that here was a man who knew his *milchik* from his *fleyshik*.)

"Yes, sir."

He waited.

"Turbulent times, sir. But a good learning opportunity."

He nodded. Then waited again. So did I.

He broke first. "Let's see, Mr. Taylor, you graduate ... "

"This spring. God willing," I added.

Meyerman chuckled at my anxiety—The old pro with the babe at his knee. He played it: "You will. I'm getting good reports on you, you know."

"Thank you, sir."

Meyerman stretched his legs as he said, "You'll do fine. I've an idea what you're going through. I'm an old Southwestern man, myself, you know."

"Go, Lynx!" I responded with a fight-song flourish of my fist, which as soon as I finished saying and doing wished I had neither said nor done.

Meyerman clapped his hands together and rubbed them briskly. "Any plans for graduate school?"

I answered truthfully. "Not at the moment, sir. I'd like to be in the field a while and find out the areas where I need to grow." *Nice.*

Meyerman smiled broadly. I smiled right back.

"Well, Jackson ... may I call you Jackson?"

And I'll call you Eddie. "Of course, sir."

He was rising; I was rising; all God's children rise when Meyerman does. "I'm so glad we had this opportunity to chat."

"Thank you, sir. Thank you for having me."

Somehow I made it through his office door, remembered to smile and thank his secretary at her polished mahogany desk in the outer office, and held steady till I was out the final door all the way to the elevator bank.

My finger found the "down" arrow and punched just as a door slid open. Cassina stood there with a handful of mail. "How was tea?" she asked as she stepped off the elevator.

"Fine," I said. "Nice ... How'd you know about that?"

Cassina stared at me with the same sort of intensity generally reserved for someone who has just farted in church. Oh. Okay. So maybe I was not quite as savvy as I originally supposed.

LAURA CONTINUED TO work at the bank, so we saw each other there and managed to have a regular lunch by ourselves (well, as by ourselves as a crowded restaurant permits) on the one day of the week when I got downtown early enough to do so.

We spent most evenings together and weekends, too, of course. At first, she seemed perfectly content to just "hang out" at the house when I needed to focus energy on studies. There were times, when after work, I would need to spend hours in the musty stacks of the library and I would come home late to find her there reading, watching television, chatting with Braden or else alone in our room waiting for me.

"I am lucky, lucky, lucky," I said to her one very late evening as we huddled together on the front porch watching an early snow.

"You are, you are, you are," she whispered—moist lips pressed gently to my ear.

MOTHER AND DAD had warned of the possibility, had feared it, they said, that my other relationships would suffer when Braden and I decided to keep the house following that first summer. The taste of freedom had been too much, I guess, and the prospect of returning to a dormitory room lacked appeal. There were few restrictions in the dorms—no curfews, etc.—but the noise and lack of privacy were not to my liking, and, against the wishes of my parents, I never returned to live in one.

My faculty advisor, when I expressed concern to him about my full schedule that semester and the subsequent pull-back from community life that it necessitated had basically asked, "What is it that you want to do?"

At the time, the fast-track seemed like such a great opportunity. A few more months work, the dreaded comprehensive exams for my major, graduation, then a sail down the river of success on Edward Meyerman's boat.

With a schedule like the one I was under, there was little time for play; therefore, friction amongst the troops as things wore on. First term exams that year ran almost smack up against Christmas. Laura planned to spend the holiday with her family in town, while Braden and I were to go to Birmingham and Knoxville respectively. By the time exams were completed, I was exhausted, I know. One look at Braden, who sported a glazed look in his eye, told me he was in much the same condition.

"God, I can't do it," I said.

Braden began to argue. "You have to, you promised."

I plopped down in a palm-patterned club chair, a recent acquisition from the Junior League Thrift Shop. "You go. It was your idea. Me, I'm here."

Braden walked around to the back of the chair and started to tip it. "Up!"

"Stop it. What the hell— "

Our words overlapped:

"She'll be here any minute."   "I'm too tired."
"She's on her way."   "I don't care. Stop it!"

"Come ... "   "Ouch."
" ... on."   "Ouch!"
"Up we go!" He tilted that chair until I fell out, landing square on my *tuchis*.

Laura walked into the room, saw us scuffling about and took on a mother's tone, "Boys! Boys! What will the neighbors think?"

"Ah! Screw the neighbors!" Braden said.

"Spoken in the true spirit of Christmas," Laura retorted.

"In or out?" Braden asked.

Car headlights flooded the room.

"She's here," sang Laura.

"Jesus Christ!"

Laura slapped me on the thigh, "Stop swearing."

"In or out, Jackson?"

"I don't care."

Braden kept on. "Your turn to decide. Look, she's coming up the driveway."

"For heaven's sake, stop her!" I said. "The way she drives she'll barrel right through the living room walls!"

"She's driving tonight, Jax."

"Braden, Braden, Braden ... " I grabbed his collar and pulled him down to me.

"Yes?"

"No, no, no," I said.

"But she insisted."

There was a rap at the door; the handle jiggled and Laura sailed toward it. "Get up, you two!"

"Braden, let me explain: She is to driving as Biffy is to riding."

"Ho! Ho! Ho!" came the familiar voice at the door.

"Do the words, 'Death-Mobile' mean anything to you?"

"Merry Christmas!" Laura said.

"Merry Christmas to you, too, honey!"

"Kiss me," said Braden.

"Mmmm-wah!" I gave my best Dinah Shore to the air.

"Lord!" said Cassina to Laura as she surveyed Braden and me on the floor. "Have you got cats?"

"Cats?" asked Laura. "No."

"Well, what dragged that mess in the house!"

"Ha! Ha!" I said snidely. "Funny as ever." Tapping my cheek, I said to her, "Buss me one right here, baby."

She did.

"Me, too! Me, too!" said Braden. They both puckered and drew within three inches of each other when the would-be kiss changed to a mutual Bronx cheer.

"Yuck!" said Laura.

Cassina and Braden exchanged a "Merry Christmas, darlin'!"

"Park it anywhere, Cassina," I said. "Take a load off."

Cassina sat on the couch. "Is this how y'all treat a lady?"

"You betcha'!" "Damn straight!" Braden and I said together.

"Well, apparently, I have come to the right place, then." She settled back.

"In or out?"

"Braden, you sound like a stuck record!"

"Then answer me, Jackson."

"All right, out! If I must be dragged kicking and screaming from my own cozy bungalow ... "

"Bung-a-what?" said Braden.

"Pig! ... then, we might as well go 'whole hog,' so to speak ... "

"Barbecue?" It was Braden's suggestion.

"Wonderful!" said Laura. "Is that all right with you, Cassina?"

"Fine."

Braden decreed, "It is done!"

"Hooray!" I said, exhausted.

"See," he said knocking me on the knee, "that wasn't so difficult, was it?"

"Bah-buh-cue!" It was Laura's turn to go off the deep end. Her voice dripped with her finest High-Southernese. "How I a-doah bah-buh-cue! And you ..." —she pointed a delicate finger at Braden—"No ... "— then to me—"may fetch it for me!"

Braden started humming "Tara's Theme."

"Y'all been at the weed, aintcha?" said Cassina.

Laura touched her hand to Cassina's, "I'm afraid," she said, still in voice, "that ah escorts to-nite ah all whacked-out from schoo-uhl."

"Can we please lay off the magnolias a bit?" I asked.

"Traitor!" cried Braden.

For once, Cassina looked dumb-founded. Divine retribution. I snickered.

"Our defenses are a bit down, Cassina," Braden explained to her.

"Good!" she said, "Then you're just in the right frame of mind!"

"Let's go," I said. "Everybody up!"

"Ye gods!" Braden whispered to me when we were on the front steps, "It's a bloody tank!"

"Cassina, where did you get this car?"

"Ain't it a beauty?" she said to me with pride. "I traded with my nephew, Russell."

"It's beautiful, Cassina," said Laura as she linked her arm through Cassina's and walked her to the driveway.

"Look at it this way, Jax. We're safe. Anything she hits will crumple like a Dixie cup."

"I heard that!" yelled Cassina.

OF THE THREE of them, the one that I was actually doing this most for was Braden. If I pulled away from campus life that year especially, there was good reason for it—understandable reason: The job as well as my relationship with Laura (who, remember, was no longer a student so we weren't in classes together, nor did she have reason to be on campus)—both things which competed mightily for my time in my priority structure.

Braden, on the other hand, seemed simply to be withdrawing, turning inward. His social life outside the arena including Laura and me had diminished significantly over the course of the last year and I have to admit, I was concerned at the change. He had always been a fun-lover (you'll recall the curfew breaker) and had developed a life outside the campus early-on our freshman year. I barely knew him then, but it being a small college, the talk (that buzzed freely about everyone) was that he had already begun dating somewhat seriously a student at the Art Academy which is located in Overton Park and which had a reciprocal agreement allowing students from each school to take classes at the other. Braden was kind of close-mouthed about it all, claiming "privacy" and in a self-mocking tone, "gallantry." I did meet an attractive young woman from there once, who escorted him to a concert in the Southwestern amphitheatre in the spring of our freshman year.

It had been about that time that our acquaintanceship had actually begun to develop. Both of us worked on the spring festival at school. It had been my advisor who was the one to suggest that I take a committee position to facilitate my own coming out of the shell. Braden chaired the committee I served on; so, through that process of meeting and work sessions, we began to discover a shared sensibility, a similar sense of humor and outlook, although it seemed otherwise that we held nothing in common: Braden, to my eighteen-almost-nineteen-mind was cosmopolitan, while I was ... oh, what's the word ... square? ... square-ish. Maybe it was the mysterious woman. Maybe it was his keen interest in art—a subject which I knew little about, unfortunately. Maybe it was practical, "two-plus-two" me in contrast to his talents—but the opposites definitely attracted till we were soon commiserating and complaining over mugs of beer the way men of that age do.

I was not "backwards" in any way at the time; however, could be more easily shocked than some. You know now that part of me changed over the years. (Where I had once seemed merely "conservative," both Braden and Laura now accused me of being "hard.")

To the contrary (of the "old me" at least), Braden met it all full in the face. I remember asking him once—it was that autumn after the strikes—I know because fall came so early that year—"What is it you want?"

He looked at me—and this, too, is something I can not forget—with those eyes of his the color of something like spring moss. Maybe we had been drinking (I'm sure we had been), but as we sat there on the grass that Thursday afternoon in a space where now a large building stands adjacent to the library, I was, for a moment, mesmerized by the color of his eyes. (Mine always get so bloodshot when I am in that condition.) The leaves of the tree behind him had all gone crimson-purple, the color of mulled-wine, and the contrast between his eyes and the tree was so palpable as to be in that instant overwhelming.

He raised his arms up with great vigor in a salute of victory and with a passionate whisper that seemed to bounce off of my sternum and reverberate against all the trees at once, exclaimed, "Everything!"

From that noble, charismatic, half-crazed knight ready to tilt at any windmill (or tulip tree) to this now much quieter soul was a remarkable difference to me. When he and the girl from the Academy broke up, he took it badly. Really hurt deeply, it seemed. He no longer dated and was rarely seen on campus outside of classes. Classmates inquired occasionally, but there had not been sufficient cause for alarm of an official nature. Apparently, he still met the two classes he did take regularly and made his assignments. But, it seemed that more and more of his time was spent in solitude.

I came home one rainy morning after class before heading downtown and found him on the partially enclosed front porch, painting. All alone. No music. Just easel, paint, brush, and him standing in the chill wind. I could not see but a glimpse of his work—something abstract, vaguely cubist, but the overall effect was depressing. He looked cold, red-nosed. Very alone. At the time, I assumed that as a result of his self-imposed seclusion, he clung to me for company. He continually pressured me to spend more time doing things together—"you know, like we used to."

Mercifully, Cassina and Braden had become thick as thieves over the course of our mutual encounters and her now routine visits to the house for supper or a weekend afternoon of music and general mischief. "Mercifully," for his sake—it provided companionship for him. "Mercifully," for me, too, for it provided something of a buffer between Cassina and me as well as Braden and me. Should Laura and I choose to be alone in a part of the house or absent altogether, there was no guilt feeling since they were now comfortable together.

Cassina claimed that it was Braden's idea that we have the Christmas adventure, while Braden maintained that Cassina was responsible. It doesn't matter, the point is we were together—something, yes, that I did look forward to for it's own value, but it also eased the nagging from Braden. Laura, when we discussed the issue (at her prompting) claimed that Braden had a legitimate beef with me—we were, after all, house-mates—"Spend a little time with him, what would it hurt?"—and that too much work made Jackson a dull boy: "What's one night off?"

So, following a barbecue supper at one of the hundreds of neon-lit establishments that have helped to earn Memphis its somewhat dubious title, "The Barbecue Capital of the World," Laura and I white-knuckled it in the back seat, while Cassina plowed her way through traffic. Braden, every other minute looking over his shoulder at us with panic-stricken, eyebrow-raised expressions, rode shotgun. Cassina simply pretended not to notice.

"How far is it, Cassina?"

"Braden, I tol' you already now, about ten more miles. Now sit still!"

We rode on for no more than five minutes.

"Cassina, how far is it?"

"Braden O'Brien, I'm gonna call your momma!"

In another two minutes we heard, "Cassina ... "

"I tell you true, you are makin' me a nervous wreck!"

Braden shot us another look.

" ... and shut up back there, you two!"

WE ARRIVED AT last to our destination. Traffic had slowed to a crawl on both sides of the highway.

"Roll down your windows, everybody!" Cassina instructed. "Now," she said after we had complied, "listen!"

It was the voice of "the king," himself, blasting the tidings from speakers hidden among the branches of trees strung with hundreds and hundreds of blue light bulbs that he was gonna' have a buh-lue Christmas.

"Ain't that somethin'?" said Cassina.

"Yes, indeed."

"My, my."

"It sure is."

TO MY SURPRISE, it was Laura who insisted that we all stop at a large strip shopping mall devoted exclusively to the selling of souvenirs before we called it a night. Never before and not since have I seen such a display.

"Somethin' for every taste," is, I believe, how Cassina summed it up.

Braden tapped me on the shoulder. In his arms, he carried a two-and-a-half foot ceramic figure.

"What the hell is that?" I asked.

"It's a cookie-jar."

Five or six dozen cookies could easily be contained in it.

"Did you ever ... "

The pompadour hair was contoured to act as a handle for the lid.

"Take it," he said.

"No, I couldn't. Really."

"G'wan!"

I reached forth with trembling hands and clutched the object. "It's breathtaking."

"What do you suppose that means?"

"What?" I asked.

"That." He pointed to some writing scrawled up the side of one leg like piping on a tuxedo. "What do you think they're trying to tell us?"

"I don't know. What's it say?"

" 'Throughout it all, I stood tall, and did it my way.' ... Oh, for Christ's sake, Jackson, don't drop it. It's your Christmas present."

"I don't know how to thank you."

Chapter Ten

*"If Your House Catch Fire,
And There Ain't No Water Roun',
If Your House Catch Fire,
And There Ain't No Water Roun',
Throw Your Trunk Out The Window,
And Let The Shack Burn Down."*
— **Traditional Blues**

BECAUSE OF ITS height, the cookie jar, by a two-thirds majority, was deemed impractical for daily use. Thus, it took it's rightful place of honor on top of the old Philco refrigerator where it stared down at us like a glassy-eyed totem.

One evening, Braden, who had volunteered to fix supper for the three of us, came into the living room where Laura sat quizzing me in preparation for a test. "I can't do it," he announced.

We both looked up at him.

"I just can't."

Laura asked him, "What's that Braden?"

"Carve up that chicken for dinner. Not with 'him' watching."

Laura hooted while my fingers rubbed my weary eyes.

On a Sunday morning (a rare moment of peace) not long after, she and I sat at the kitchen table drinking coffee and reading the paper—Laura with the comics, me with the business section, of course.

"He's right, you know."

"Who's right?"

"Braden."

"About what?"

"Even with my back turned ... " A *frisson* ran through her body.

"What's wrong?"

"Gives me the heebie-jeebies."

I took the coffee cup from her hand. "No more of that for you, my angel."

IT WAS MY final semester and I was bearing down hard: Studying for "comps"—mandatory within my major, as well as a half-time work week at the bank and a full load of classes. I had bitten off more than I could chew; but stubborn or prideful, I was determined not only to chew it, but to swallow also.

Again, the three of us were at the kitchen table. I had books in stacks and three-by-five note cards all over. Crumpled paper wads lay about on the floor and those raggedy, confetti-like edges of paper that come loose from spiral-bound notebooks when their leaves are yanked from them stuck to the blue velour bathrobe I wore.

"Jackson, listen to me." Laura stroked my hand. "Enough's enough. You need to go to bed."

"I can't go to bed yet. I have to finish this. If I don't write at least three more pages tonight, I'll never finish."

"You can finish it tomorrow." It was a plea. Her hand gripped mine. "Jackson —!"

Oh, those eyes of hers! Unfair! My defense against them was anger. "Will you stop it!" She gripped tighter. I wrestled my hand from hers. "I told you, I have a schedule! If I don't stick to it, everything will fall apart." In my obsession to have everything on the menu, this young wide-eyed fool forgot something valuable (and if it's not in the lyrics of some blues song somewhere, it ought to be): You don't have to work to get what you already have, but maybe you better work on keeping it.

Her hand hit the table. "You and your schedule! I swear to God, you can't stop. That's it, isn't it? You *can't* stop!"

"Oh for God's sake, Laura! Stop being so melodramatic. Christ, that really pisses me off!"

Braden toyed with a pack of cigarettes on the table in front of him.

"Give me one of those," I barked at him.

"Yas-suh, massah," he snapped. "You wants me to smoke it fo' yuz, too?" He took a cigarette and dangled it from the end of his lips.

"Cut that out and give me a god-damned cigarette!"

He left the pack where it sat in front of him. "Get it yourself."

"Don't you ever study?" I asked.

"It's all done," he said. "All but my senior project." The smile on his face was forced. His mouth pushed upwards. "And I'm putting the finishing touches on that."

"Well, bully for you, Braden."

Without speaking, he rose from the table and walked towards the window near the sink.

I reached for a cigarette. After I had taken a couple of drags, I said to them, "Look, I'm sorry. Okay? I promise, when all this is over, we'll all go do something nice again. Just us."

"Cassina, too?" Laura asked.

"Sure. If you like."

She sat very still. After a moment, a small voice came from her, "You've become like a monster, Jackson. Voracious. Eating up everything in sight."

My lips twisted. *What's gotten into them?* I turned to Braden who was busy studying the cookie-jar. "Look, Third Term should be a breeze. We can enjoy each other's company. The weather will be nice." (At that time, Southwestern had a trimester system that consisted of two twelve-week terms and a short six-week term. It's uniqueness lay in the fact that the third term wasn't a winter interim, but rather a more relaxed, freer April-May period whose purpose was exploration of non-traditional subjects or concentrated small tutorials. I don't know about now, but then, they did their level best to prevent the kind of rigidity that I was getting trapped in.)

Braden asked me, "What are you planning on taking Third Term?"

"A Shakespeare class—his later plays—*The Tempest*, that sort of thing."

Braden's face brightened.

"And an individualized study ... "

"Yeah?"

"Kenyesian Economic Theory for the Late Twentieth Century."

His face sank and he turned away. "You know, it's amazing," Braden said. He studied the cookie-jar intently.

"What's that?" I asked.

"How his eyes sort of follow you around the room."

"Spooky, isn't it?" said Laura.

"That's it!" I jumped up and ran to the refrigerator, grabbed the container, and headed towards the back door.

"Where are you going?" Braden asked.

"To bury this frigging thing in the back yard."

"Won't do you any good," Braden said, "come spring, he'll just rise from the dead."

I looked at Laura still sitting at the table. Her question, unspoken, hung in the air between us.

"Look, right now, I just want to finish an Honor's Thesis."

"Phi Beta Kappa not enough for you, genius?" she snapped.

We stared at each other without speaking.

"Besides," Braden continued his line of thought, "you'll have trouble digging up that frozen ground ... "

"What do you mean?"

"Look, kids, it's snowing."

I bolted to the window. "How can it be snowing? It's too late in the season for snow!"

Both Braden and Laura came to the window and smiled.

"Damn," I said, setting the cookie-jar down roughly on the counter. "You know what it's like to get around this half-assed town in the snow! This is just what

I need," I said sardonically. My hands gripped the edge of the sink. "Thanks a lot, God!"

What is it I hear now, all these years later as I look back and listen? Is it a voice? Is it merely a breeze—the wind? Something. Something. Something whispering softly as the snow, "You're welcome."

🙶🙶🙶

I TOLD YOU early on that this would not be the story you want to hear told as you want to hear it. I can only tell you what I know, my impressions. Think of this story, maybe, as if it were painted by Monet. When it's over, stand far away and perhaps you'll see what it truly is. That is what I am trying to do even still.

Who can honestly say what causes relationships to change, what the myriad forces are that tug on individuals? Gravity from within, gravity outside, entities—undiscovered, unknown, unknowable?—planets. Seasons, tides, rhythms. Sometimes it's in the air as potent as the weather. Something known, yet unvoiced, unsaid, unspoken. Fear? Is it fear that keeps us quiet? Fear of ... change. Fear of the unknown—that which is to come—that which is beyond our control. The inevitable. Fear of ... being right. Of being wrong. Of heart break. God-damn you, Braden O'Brien, even now in my mind's eye, I see you standing there.

That intangible thing hovered in the air that month thick as the humidity of a Memphis July as Second Term and Winter turned to Third and Spring. Plans to graduate from college. Smiles masking sad souls of students who would soon part—"commence" was the official word—

not really knowing, not fully understanding that they would never return, not really return. Could not.

Career plans discussed. Jobs waiting for some already; others still waiting or searching. Hoping.

Impending disaster. Something dying, defying Spring. Yes. No. *What am I doing here?*

My Honors Thesis was accepted. Mother and Dad were excited—planned to drive over for baccalaureate and graduation—no, "commencement"—of course. Was there anything special I wanted to do? No, not really? A fine dinner, at least. Okay. The Peabody Hotel? Well, of course. No Mother's-Son-of-the-South would be anyplace else. Guests? Oh, Laura, certainly. No, no, I think his parents are coming up from Birmingham. Yes, I'll check. Anybody else? No.

The plans at "Pleasant Hill"—why did we call it that?—that sounds so *dumb*—the plans were to stay on. Both of us. That is, Braden and myself. Laura was a constant fixture. Legal residence still with Mom and Dad over near M.S.U. A good thing. A steady thing. Yes, yes, that's what we have. Well, yes, I feel the same way. You know that. Sure, sure.

Jobs. Me at the bank. Full-time just as soon as I wanted. How about July 1? A little time off for good behavior, ha! ha! Fine, great. Laura, also at the bank continuing on her track. Braden painting, painting, painting! Not yet ready to go solo as an artist. What about a job at the museum? Someone else's gallery? Hard to come by. Not for you, kiddo, surely.

Boom, boom, boom. Days going by. Now flying. I'm leaving something out. Something's missing. Letters to write—professors, thank you's. A little something for the advisor, nothing too much. People to see. I can't, I'm sorry—have to work. Friday night? Sure! Great! Love to! Invitations! God,—I forgot—how could I be so stupid! What else?

Zoom. Like a jet. Gone. Distant echo. Did I miss it all? Gone.

Phone call. Out of the sky. A phone call from a recruiter for a large bank in Boston.

"Mr. Taye-lah?"

"Yes?"

"This is Rebecca Cranston."

"Yes?"

"We met at Recruitment Day at yuah college in February."

"Uh ... "

"From Bah-stun ... ?"

"Oh, yes! Uh ... good morning. How are you?"

"Fine, thank you. And yuh-self?"

"Very good, thanks."

Recruitment Day?

"Go," my advisor had encouraged me.

"But I have a job already. The bank. Meyerman."

"A formality. Good practice. Give 'em a little competition. Why not?"

"Mr. Taye-lah. It appeahs we may be having an opening soon and weah wonduhring if you might be intarested in tahking fuhthah."

What a voice! "Ah! Miss Cranston, I'm afraid I'm already committed. I've secured a full-time spot with my present employer."

"I see, Mr. Taye-lah. Well, we wah cuhtainly impressed with yuah academic recahd and with you, puhsahnally—yuah achieeevemuhnts ... "

It's the Tower of Babel, I live in, isn't it? "Thank you, Miss Cranston, I certainly appreciate that, but ... "

"So, shall we set an appointment?"

I couldn't believe how interested she was. Or how pushy for that matter. Yankee pluck?

"Miss Cranston, I'm graduating from college in two weeks."

"I'm shuah it's a busy time foah you, Mr. Taye-lah ... "

"Yes, yes, it is."

"We can fly you up on Sunday night and have you back in Memphis by Monday evening, oah would you prefuh just a day trip?"

"No, no, Sunday night is fine ... " I could call in sick for once to the bank, bag the Keynesian gig.

"Wonduhful! Weah vewee eagah to meet with you ..."

Obviously. This is too good to be true. And why not? Why not at least "he-ah" what they have to say?

Everything was expertly set up and we hung up. I couldn't believe this! I rang my faculty advisor at school. "Mackie! Jackson Taylor. You'll never believe what just happened."

"Go, Jackson," Braden said. "Why not? If nothing else you have a free trip, some baked beans ... "

"For once in your life, you're right, Braden." I grabbed him around the collar in a headlock. "Sometimes you're okay."

"Hey, tanks a-lot!"

"Sure. Or as they say in 'Bah-stun' ... 'shu-ah'."

"Party Saturday, remember?"

"Oh, right! I almost forgot. Perfect," I said, "perfect timing. A *bon voyage* for me! Let's see, I better put in a few hours at the bank Saturday morning ... Perfect!"

Braden grinned. "It is. It is, it is."

🍂🍂🍂

LAURA FRANKLIN STOOD in the inner doorway of "Pleasant Hill" that Saturday. Her hair cascaded—that is the only word for it—cascaded down to her shoulders in splashes of amber. I drew a deep breath. She noticed me there as she stood in the archway between the dining room and living room. For a moment her eyes dropped and a finger twirled lazily in a wave of hair as if she were a girl again. She raised her silvery blue eyes slowly until they met mine and I knew at once she was not. No.

I stepped forward as she did, her hand extending slowly, then her left reached up to clutch around my shoulder. She fixed me firmly in her gaze and spoke my name as if it were a commandment, "Jackson Taylor."

"Laura."

Her hand clutched more tightly against my shoulder, then she was kissing me. As she did, I breathed in the fragrance from her.

"Honeysuckle?"

She did not respond to me, but turned to Braden. "See, I told you he'd come. Didn't I, Braden?"

I looked to see him standing there against the arch, darkness behind him, where a moment ago she had been.

"Honeysuckle?" I asked again.

"Don't you like it?" she said.

"Yes, but honeysuckle isn't in bloom yet. It's too early."

"You can get it from a florist if you call around," Braden suggested.

Then it hit and it was my turn to fix a gaze.

He noticed it, I know, because something small changed then around the lines of his cheeks just to the sides of his nostrils.

My lips arranged themselves into a tight smile and I felt my eyes crinkle.

"Hello, darling," she said as she kissed me on the cheek again.

My arm encircled her waist. "Hello, there," I said to her. All the while, I kept my eyes on his.

"See, Braden," she said again. "I told you he'd come."

🍎🍎🍎

Chapter Eleven

The Tennessee Waltz
(Version Interruptus)

INTERRUPTING MY LONG reverie and closing the *déjà vu* loop, Laura said, "Well, Jackson, I'm certainly glad to see you, too, although," (and now her training as a perfect Southern lady shone at its brightest) "I wish the circumstances of our reunion were different."

Right then, I wished I had never come, despite how much she "knew" that I would; but knowing my place (taught early and taught well), I fell right into the polite word dance known as "The Tennessee Waltz" as naturally and as easily as ... as easily as falling off a ... well ... Anyway, here is how it's done: Step One: Agree—"Yes, so do I, of course;"—then up the ante slightly, to whit—"It's terrible, isn't it?"

"Yes, yes, it certainly is." Step Two: The lady leads—Laura glided to the sofa and perched on one end. She extended her right hand, palm up. "Please —" Braden and I both took seats—dutiful as the Tarleton twins—he in the chair, I at the other end of the couch.

Step Three: Talk about anything, but never, ever about what's really going on—"I'm afraid I can't be staying long. I had no idea how late it was!" (I had dropped in unannounced, sponged a meal, and now, the least I could do would be to stick him with the dishes.) And punctuate, always punctuate with giddy laughter.

"Nonsense," Laura said. "It's early yet. And it's never too late for an old friend."

"How sweet of you." (Count: One-two-three, one-two-three. One-two-three, one-two-three. Now dance.) "And how well you're looking."

"Thank you, Jackson. My goodness, but why are you sitting so far away?"

Because, I'm afraid of trippin' over that big ol' hoop skirt you slipped into when I watn't lookin', honeychile. "Let's just say I feel safer over here. Ha! ha! ha! ha! ha-ha!" I looked to Braden. *Oh, let's bring you in on this, too, old sport, make it a real menage a trois.* "Ha-ha. Ha-ha. Ha! Ha! Ha!"

He jumped right in. "Ha, ha, ha."

Atta' boy! We looked at Laura.

Her head tipped back. "Ha, ha, ha, ha-ha, ha-ha!"

And they're off!

"Braden, have you offered Jackson anything to drink?"

"We've had supper!" I exclaimed.

"Supper?" She stressed the word the same way Cassina said "coffee."

I shook my head "yes" and just about slapped my thigh.

Braden's turn: "Yes, supper."

Laura: "No!"

Braden: "*Yes*, I tell you!"

What the fuck is so hard to understand about "supper"?!

Laura again: "Oh, my, I wish I had known."

"It was a surprise to me, too."

My turn! "Yes, I'm afraid I did a terrible thing."

"What's that?" Laura asked.

"I just dropped in without calling. And, of course, Braden here," (leading with the wrist, my graceful sweeping arm extends to him) "was 'gallant' enough—ha! ha!—to offer to make dinner."

"Don't be silly. It was nothing."

"It was ... " I turned to Laura, " ... a terrible imposition on my part, I'm afraid."

She said, "Circumstances such as these warrant unconventional behavior."

A triple head maneuver: 1. I smiled at her. 2. I looked to him. 3. Wrinkling my brow in quizzical form, I turned back to her.

Tap dance: "What I *mean* ... " she started.

And now for a brief, but heartfelt *pas de deux:*

"It was," said Braden, "just like old times."

"It was at that," I genuinely agreed.

"Yes."

"Thank you."

"You're welcome."

One, two, three. One, two, three. One, two, three. One, two, three.

"Jackson," said Laura. "How long will you be in town?"

"A week. Ten days at most."

"Unless, of course—" said Braden.

"Cassina turns up."

"Of course," said Laura.
"Of course," I echoed.

"Well, let's hope ... "
"Yes."
"Here's to."

"Braden, have you heard anything more?"
"Nothing new, Laura."
"Discouraging."

"What do you suppose has happened, Jackson?"
"I have no idea, Laura."
"None?"
"How would I?"
"Well, yes ... "
"Yes," said Braden.

"I hope it's nothing awful," she led.
"God forbid," said I.
"Don't tempt fate."

"Jackson, what are you doing?"
"Me? Nothing."
"Oh."

"You're teaching now, aren't you?"
"Yes. Yes, I am."
"The job at the bank ... ?"

"Didn't work out."
"Sorry."
"Me, too."

"Me, three."
"Ha! Ha! Ha!"
"Ha! Ha! Ha!"

"Jackson, is something wrong?"
"No, Laura, nothing."
"Sure?"

A single waltz-clog from her: "Braden, how-was-your-day?"
Now him; I wait. "Fine. Did I tell you ... ?"
"What?"
"That bank Out East ... "
"What?"
"Loves the murals."

And again: "Great! Jackson, what are you looking at?"
"Your head, Laura."
"My head?"
"Yes. I'm looking for the scar."
"What scar?"
"From where they liposuctioned your brain."

Rip. Scratch. Needle off.

"Well, that didn't take long," she said.
"I'm sorry."
"Fine."
"Braden, forgive me. That was rude." I stood to go.
They made no effort to stop me until I had already opened the wooden door and pushed at the screen one.

"Jackson, wait— " Braden's voice.

I waited. "I'm sorry."

"Tomorrow—"

"And tomorrow and tomorrow ... " I couldn't help it.

He waited. "Come by the studio. Tomorrow afternoon. We'll go look around."

"I'm going tomorrow morning to do some checking."

"We'll look together. How 'bout it?"

I looked to Laura still sitting on the couch. She did not speak, but looked at me and nodded a small "yes."

"Time?"

"Three o'clock?"

"Okay ... Braden, I —"

He held up his hand—a stop sign. "Three o'clock."

The door closed behind me.

Not ready to go back to the hotel yet, I got in the car and drove downtown, climbed the sweeping curve of the on-ramp to the Hernando DeSoto Bridge and crossed the river to Arkansas looking down into the black water below me. There's nothing over there in Arkansas until you get past the first levee and honestly, not a whole lot after that. I stopped for hot biscuits and a cup of coffee at a truck stop in West Memphis. It was an old trick I had learned years ago: No matter how blue you feel, nothing will make you feel better than driving back to Memphis—viewing it from a different perspective—and seeing the lights on that side reflected in the deep river.

Chapter Twelve

And _That's_ What I Like About The South

I HAD BROKEN the rules: The rules of polite society. Polite society was not a thing, though, that I remembered any of us particularly just aching to dwell in. In fact, so much of the time that we had lived in was about breaking "the rules," writing our own. Who was it who had been chastised for being "too conservative," "too rigid"? Brutal honesty and "do your own thing" had been the watchwords of the day. Relaxation. Nevertheless, there was still a code—even in our own little brave new world around Southwestern (though I am certain that I may not have realized it as such then)—of "protection" and I have learned it and its value over the years. Honor. When push comes to shove, protect the ones you love. The fact remained, however, that we were now all grown up. Not twenty, but rapidly approaching twice that. I lost sight of it for a moment. It was no longer 1980.

Every civilized culture has its own ways of dealing with thorny situations and transgressors. The South has several particular catch-phrases, *bons mots*, that come into play in such situations. Among these are:

"Well, I'll be!"; "What about it, what about it!"; and the ever-useful "Bless your heart!" C.Y.A. (if you know what I mean) as well as you're loved one's. We're all in this together. When in doubt, provide ambiguity. Let the other person appear to be correct.

So—without a doubt, Laura was right and I was wrong. Hers was the high-road; she chose to take it. I, the interloper, should have followed, whether or not I found such an extreme course appropriate or necessary.

Another slice of Humble Pie? Who me? Well, my goodness, I couldn't really. Thank you just the same. Oh well, perhaps just a sliver.

May I apologize again for my despicable behavior? I was in gravest error. (The truth, plain and simply spoken, can be a mighty thing.)

Now that you know both The Code and The Waltz, if you think about it, you will understand the rest of the story. I hereby re-sheath my two-edged sword and remove my hand. Suicide shall not be necessary. O, Chivalry, where is thy sting?

The Southern Rules for men together are different (and change as the number gathered grows). Braden, you might think, would be perfectly justified in punching me in the nose. Instead, he chose to invite me to his studio the next day and then join me in my search—which would become our search—for Cassina Gambrel. Braden O'Brien is a gentleman in the truest sense.

HE SHOWED ME around his art studio and gallery in a converted Midtown storefront near Overton Square. "The location's good. We get the tourist spillover, but I'm thinking of opening an annex further out, maybe even closing this place down eventually."

That is when I learned the facts about the boom of East Memphis and the suburbs. Apparently, I had just seen the beginnings in my few forays years ago.

"That's where the money is. The big money, at least in the highest concentration." Braden's physical appearance reflected his newfound (to me) attraction to money. He was a man in his late thirties, but he dressed like a college "preppy"—something I'd never witnessed him do before. From his tortoise-shell glasses to his penny loafers, he was all casual-chic.

"Who can blame you?" I asked.

"It's a business like any other when all is said and done."

"Yep."

"Ready to go?"

Bet your ass. "Sure am!"

The gallery was left in the hands of one of two employees which he also told me he now had working for him. "Plus, a student intern from our old college."

"They changed the name. Sold out."

"Marketing."

"What's in a name? Ha! Ha!"

We got in the car (my car, or rather, the rental company's) and headed west. (I did not tell him about my excursion the night before.)

"Any luck this morning?" he asked me as we drove.

"Not really. I headed out early, made the synagogue and yeshiva tour thinking the police might not have considered that. She still catered on occasion I found out."

Braden confirmed it. "Yes. Although I don't really know why," he said. "To keep her hand in, I guess. By this time, she didn't need the money, I'm sure."

"Cassina had money?"

"I don't think she was loaded, but I think she was comfortable."

"Braden —"

"Meyerman appreciated her loyalty."

"Sure. Braden—"

"I expect she was well fixed."

"Braden—"

"What?"

"Why are we talking about her in the past tense?"

He shrugged.

"Can we not?"

He shrugged once more.

"Anyway, I found out that not only had the police been there, but a private detective had already questioned just about everyone."

"It's nice to have connections, I guess."

There was a pause while I tried to think what to say next. "The gallery—"

"Yes?"

"I meant to tell you ... "

"What?"

"Nice. Very impressive."

"Thanks."

"And your work ... beautiful."

"It is, isn't it?"

"Egotist."

"Well, if I don't blow my own ... "

"Yeah, well, used to be an ordinance against that in this city, you know."

"What's that?"

I gave two quick taps of the car horn with the heel of my hand. "Blowing your own. Horn, I mean. Ha!"

"Really?"

"Yes."

"Hmm. Imagine."

I remembered the hordes of tourists that Cassina and I had seen that August. "Still as many fans as there used to be?"

"More," he said. "You wouldn't believe it."

"Really?"

"Really. It's an industry. Big bucks. Major."

"No kidding?"

"Seriously. It's the best thing he ever did for the city."

"Lot of new buildings down here," I said. "I hardly recognize the place anymore."

"No, it's not the city you once knew."

"It sure ain't."

We turned and drove past Court Square. People on the benches. Pigeons.

"Wait a minute," I want to say to him. "Who is that over there?" I want to say, "Who is that woman and who is that boy?" I want to say. I want to say. But my jaw is tight, my throat constricted, my tongue swollen and heavy in my mouth lies there like so much tonnage. It's as if I've been struck dumb, mute as the moon caught in eternal "O"-gaping grief.

My jaw works mechanically and turning to him, at last I can stammer, "Th-that ... that looks like—"

"What?" he says.

But when I turn back, they are gone like that.

"It's a little cold to be sitting outside yet, isn't it?" Braden pointed to two people sitting near the edge of the square, one gesturing animatedly.

"Nah. In Boston, they'd be running around in their shirt-sleeves."

"Crazy New Englanders," he said.

"Reckon so," I said. "Pretty soon, though, it'll be too hot to be out there."

"Who would that stop?"

"Say, wait a minute," Braden said. "You really wanta' see something that'll blow your mind? Drive north a little more."

A few minutes later we were there. "What is it?" I asked him.

"What does it look like, *schmuck*?" (We had learned only the best Yiddish from Cassina.)

"A pyramid. I saw it when I flew in."

Braden's face lit up. "Thirty-two stories."

"No kiddin'?"

"Yes," he said with pride. "That makes it the third largest pyramid in the world."

"Gee-whiz."

"It's a stadium."

"Oh ... Well, why'd they build it down in that lowland?"

Braden laughed. "There's been some talk about that. But you know Memphis. False-modesty. They can't quite work it up to be audacious: Put it on a bluff where it can be seen and all. You know, make a real landmark for the world to see."

"Mmm."

"Light under a bushel," he explained. "We're shy."
"Braden—"
"And look over there. Mud Island. All built up."
"I don't want to know."
He ignored me. "People live over there now."
Shut up, Braden. "Braden—"
"Expensive condos."
"Braden, I don't recognize anything anymore."
"Incredible, isn't it? Yep. We're all grown up."
"It sure seems that way, doesn't it?"
"Yes."

"Braden—"
"What, Jackson?"
"Where are we going?"
"I don't have a god-damn clue."

"How about a drink?"
"I sure as hell could use one," he said.
"Me, too. In some out of the way place where nobody knows me and I won't see a soul. No dancing allowed."
"I know just what you mean ... Jackson—"
"Great ... What?"
"Turn here," he said.
"Where? Here?"
"No. I know just the place."
"Great!"
"Jackson?"
"What is it?"
"You're going the wrong direction."
I sure am Braden.
🙞🙞🙞

THE BAR WE finally arrived at and now sat in had absolutely no atmosphere. Not even a bad one. Wooden paneling. Dark. Tables and chairs. If there was a jukebox, somebody had the good sense not to play it.

"This is perfect," I said as we started on our third. "How'd you ever find it?"

"I don't know," he said. "I stumbled upon it one day. I got lucky. 'Ya rolls de dice. Ya takes yo'r chances.' It's quiet. My own little sanctuary. No one knows about it."

"I swear to God I won't tell a soul. 's our secret."

"So, Jackson, you haven't told me yet. How's the old love life?"

"You wanta know the truth?" I asked him.

"Of course not," he said. He raised his mug and we clinked.

"Well, you little son-of-a-bitch, I'm gonna' tell you anyway."

"Oh, goodie—"

"There is no one. Absolutely no one at all."

"Aww come on," Braden said. "Are you tryin' to tell me that in all of that great frozen territory called Boston ... that is above the Arctic Circle, isn't it? ... that there's nobody at all? That in all these years ... "

"Snap out of it, Braden. Of course, there's been one or two, here or there. Some serious, some not at all. But no one that's—you know."

"Yep."

"Well, something was missing."

"I hear you." He toasted me with his mug and took a long swallow.

"Here's what I think, Braden, if you want to know what I think—not that you do, of course, and I know you think that. Because basically, no one really cares about what anybody else thinks; so when they ask that: 'Do you want to know what I think?'—it's just rhetorical, because nobody does. But here it is anyway: I think ... " I peered over my beer mug. "I think that everybody gets one great love in their life and sometimes you get it soon on so you can get it out of the way and get on with what's really unimportant in life."

We clinked again.

"And the bank—?"

"I hated it."

"Ahhhh ...." he said.

"Hated it, absolutely."

"I see." He leaned back and pressed his fingertips together. "But it looked like such a tremendous opportunity ..."

"Braden, stop that. I hate that little thing you do."

"What thing?"

"That wise-Buddha thing. Cut it out, okay?"

"Okay."

"So, I had this 'tremendous opportunity' after a couple of years to get a Masters. Part-time. The bank would pay half. A perk. Lucky me. I took it."

"A chance."

"Why not?" I said.

"Why not!" he echoed.

"Amen."

"Up yours." We drank.

"And before long, I picked up an assistance—assist—assistanceship. That's the word! (Damn these cheap wooden teeth.) And one thing led to another ... The little ball rolled around the wheel of fortune and ... "

"And ... " he said.

"And there was an opening at a small school—a liberal arts college."

"So?"

"Exactly. So I said 'bumpf' to the bank and off I went. Income cut by two thirds."

"Good boy!" Braden said with a slap to my shoulder.

"Hooray for me! Not that I was looking to replicate the past or anything ... "

"Nah, of course not."

We sat for about five full minutes without speaking. Five full minutes is an amazingly long time for people to spend in silence, especially after they have not spoken for about fifteen years. *So, what's five more minutes?*

I spoke first. "But you know what, Braden, old ... friend?"

"What's that, Jackson?"

"I hate it."

"Mmm."

"Hate it. It and Boston and life, I think."

"More than you hate Memphis?" he asked.

"But I don't ... I don't ... " I conceded at last—"Love-hate. Jeez! I never thought about it like that before. Love-hate."

"But you went to Boston ... "

"What choice did I have?"

"Probably ... " He stopped to think. " ... Probably not much."

"I remember ... "
"Mm-hmm," he said, "so do I."

WHAT WE REMEMBERED then was the Saturday before I left for the interview. Partying, as promised. Laura, Braden, Cassina, me. Spring. Stereo up full-volume. Beautiful Memphis in May. Doors open, windows raised. Those breezes blowing and the redbud trees shaking.

Cassina and I busied ourselves at the kitchen counters, choppin' and slicin'. Not a melon in sight.

"Hey, Cassina. Reminds me of old times, huh?"

"Ye gods!" she said. "If I ever made a mistake, that was it!"

"Oh, come on, we weren't that bad." My honor as a *schlep* was at stake here.

"Sheesh!"

Someone changed the record to an old blues singer who was at that time making a big comeback.

"God, she's great," I said. I danced around the kitchen and sang along. Cassina chopped. "What's the matter, Cassina? You don't like her?"

"Old has-been," Cassina grumbled.

"Aww come-on. Give the old girl a break. Let her have her place in the sun."

"Disgusting."

"She's fun."

Cassina made that sniffy face of hers like she smelled something bad.

I shuffled towards her. "You're just jealous."

"Ha!" she exclaimed.

"Jealous. I know."

She sneered at me.

"Cassina, I bet you're a good blues singer," I said.

"What's that?" asked Braden, entering the room and heading for the refrigerator. "You say Cassina's a singer? I've never heard you sing, Cassina." He retrieved a can of Stroh's and popped the top.

"Come on, Cassina, sing us the blues," I chimed in.

Cassina slammed her open hand against the pink formica counter-top. "I am not a singer. I don't sing!"

I jumped in stunned response.

"If y'all wanna hear somebody sing the blues, go to one of those clubs downtown!" she continued vehemently.

A quick glance at Braden—he looked just as shocked as I was. "Cassina, I ... " But she did not let me finish.

"I swear to God! I don't know where you people ever got the notion that all black people are goin' aroun' singin' the blues all the time!"

"Cassina, I ... "

She looked straight at me and said, "You people are jus' too goddamn Romantic!" With that, she turned furiously, almost bumping into Braden. She gave the swinging door a great "bam" with the heal of her hand and shouldered through it with all the force of an asteroid crashing through the atmosphere.

The door swung back behind her noisily, then forward again before settling to its place.

" 'You people. You people'," I said, mocking her. I didn't know what she meant by "you people," but she said it twice and it stung like a hornet.

Braden, seemingly recovering a little, said, "What in the hell was that?"

"The bitch. That fucking bitch!" I went for another beer and slammed the refrigerator door so hard that the lid on the ceramic Elvis clattered.

Never one to let go easily, after two beats I followed her through the door. The music had stopped. I trounced through the dining room full of righteousness, full of indignation, to the living room, where Cassina and Laura stood near the door engaged in a whispered exchange.

"Cassina!" It was a forceful call whose ferocity startled even me. "Cassina Gambrel!"

Both she and Laura now stared at me as if I had gone completely off my rocker.

"Cassina Gambrel, I'm mad at you."

It was Laura, not Cassina, who spoke next. "Jackson Taylor, how dare you!"

Her words were like a blow, some unexpected left hook. I staggered, then recovering, shot back. "Me? ... Me! You've got it backwards."

"I don't think so, Jackson." She placed her hands on both of Cassina's shoulders in a gesture of protection. "She told me what you said."

Now I was on the defensive. "*I* said! Cassina, have you flipped your lid completely?"

She turned from me quickly.

Laura spoke again. "You've hurt her, Jackson. Can't you see that?"

Furious. Furious! Rage poured from me: "God damn it! God damn it and you, too! I am not going to take it. Not from you and not from that ... that ... "

Now it was Cassina's turn. Quietly, directly, she turned her head, looked me straight in the eye and said, "That *what*, Jackson?"

I was silent, but only long enough for the boiling to begin again, slowly, steadily, "You filthy, despicable..."

Her voice shot out of her, topping mine. "That's it! I'm outta' here!"

She broke from Laura and ran through the open door.

"Damn!" I swore again. "Damn it to hell!"

Laura stood glaring at me. "Well, Mr. Taylor. I do hope you're satisfied." The proverbial straw.

"You go to hell." I went back to the kitchen looking for a beer, a cigarette. *No,* I thought, *no, this is too important.* Oh, the drama. Oh, the passion.

When I got back to the living room, Laura was at the door, keys in hand. As she left, with one brief look at me, she said, "You talk to him, Braden. I'm leaving."

She was gone and I turned to Braden. With an acerbic (and exasperated) laugh I said, "What happened? Did everybody get their 'monthly visitor' suddenly?"

"That's not funny, Jackson."

"What happened—did you get yours, too?" I sneered.

"Do you blame her? Do you blame either of them?"

"Great, Braden. That's just great. This is what I really need. I thought we were gonna' have a party. Everybody be relaxed. Happy. Isn't that what y'all wanted?"

"Not when you're acting like that."

"Wait a minute, wait a minute!" Now I really was confused. "You were in there a minute ago. You saw what happened. Everything was going along just fine. Then wham!"

Braden stood there by the fireplace with his arms to his sides.

"See, you can't say anything." The tone in my voice was accusing.

"Now you listen to me, Jackson, and you listen good. You have been running around here driving everyone crazy with your climbing, with your obsessions—trying to fill up something empty in you by making everyone or everything into an image or a symbol."

I scoffed at him. "You been takin' a course in Psych. 101 when my back was turned, Braden?"

He paid no attention. "*That's* what was missing," he said. "Cassina Gambrel was missing."

"Now you're the one making her a symbol." I tried turning the tables. "You know she would hate that!" I protested.

"Exactly!" he said. "That's exactly what I'm talking about."

I was lost. "Braden, what the hell *are* you talking about? 'Cause I don't get it!"

"Cassina is not a symbol. Cassina is Cassina. Cassina is a person, plain and simple ... "

"Braden, I don't know where you are coming from with this—"

"Stop turning everything into an event. Every moment, every thing. Life is life. Not everything is so momentous or full of meaning!"

"I know that."

"No, you don't! You keep thinking you do, keep saying you do, but you really don't."

"Fuck you."

"Now there's a fine answer," he retorted. "And something you've said once too often, Jackson."

"What do you want?"

"For you to see what the problem really is. You keep pigeon-holing her. Trying to make her more than she is or ever was. It's that goddamn Mr. Super-Man, I'm-so-together thing you do. You want to be an over-achieving Mr. New South so much that you become a caricature! You can't just 'be' and let things be! Be as they really are!"

"You bastard!" I yelled at him as I slumped into the armchair.

"I'm right, you know. For once, I'm right. For Christ's sake, I am so tired of stereotypes. Stereotypes of 'liberals,' stereotypes of 'rednecks,' stereotypes of the 'pained Southerner'—black or white—who has 'come so far, worked so hard to throw off the heavy yoke of oppression.' For God sakes, nobody can live anymore. If I hear one more time or read one more novel about a white-trash girl—'I wuz a artist an' they dint know, an' so they set out to murder mah very soul'—or one more valiant, suffering Negro—'He swam the yellow waters of the mighty Mississippi to save the lives of the very one's who despised him, for their own sake and the sake of all his brethren' or whatever—I think I will puke! Puke, do you hear me? Vomit up my Confederate gray guts! I'm drowning in Southerness, drowning in Memphis! And you—you are living in a dream world, Jackson ... "

"*Me?!*"

"You want to put Cassina in that world, in that mold: 'It is a tale told by an idiot;' 'I have lost much, Cyra'—'Look for it no more, it is gone with the wind!' It is gone. If it ever *was*! I, myself, have never worn pantaloons and a hoop-skirt. And Cassina, God bless her, if she is symbolic of anything, is a symbol of the one person in your world who is *not* a symbol. She is a free *spirit*. A great *soul*. A free-radical who does not compute in your narrow confines."

Where was this coming from? The feel of it all was that he was improvising; but even amidst all the grandstanding, there was just enough of some little thing in his words that rang as true as a bell, slapping me in the face with their sound—and boy did I hate him for it: Remember Step Three.

Braden's words soared out of him, "Will you please stop trying so hard to be a fount of wisdom, to be 'right' and 'perfect'. Just be like the rest of us. There are thousands, millions, of Southern people, Northern people, all kinds of people, getting up, going to work, coming home, eating, sleeping, and rutting our lives away every day. And each and every one of us is an individual. Not some 'vision' you may be having at the moment!"

Ouch. I started towards him.

"Back off, Jackson!" he commanded. The sound came from deep within him. I had never heard him use that much force before. "You're too close."

Now it was my turn to grab keys and leave.

I crashed that night on a couch in a social room at the college, looking out the window and up at the tower. "A modern-day Icarus ... " *What am I doing here? It's time to go.* The next day, I returned home—no one was there, thank God—packed a suitcase and left for the airport in Boston.

WITH THAT MEMORY finished, "Braden," I said to him in the bar, "did you ever look back and suddenly realize that maybe you got it all wrong?"

BRADEN AND I arrived at the restaurant on Beale Street something shy of sober. He had asked, said she wanted to see me, my option, an olive branch. How could I decline?

Laura thanked me for joining them as we took our seats. "I'm glad you could come, Jackson." Simply stated.

"Why, madam," I whipped out a trowel and laid on my best Colonel Beauregard Andrew Jackson Taylor, C.S.A., accent. "I know the ways of the South. Never forget, I pray thee, that I am one of her truest sons."

Braden chuckled and I continued, "How often I have sucked at her very bosom. Oh, pardon me, did I say that? What I meant to say, of course, was 'tit'."

Laura had the grace to cut a laugh, which, if not entirely genuine, was a reasonable enough facsimile thereof. "We wanted you to see what they've done down here," Laura said.

"They've certainly been busy," I said. "As I recall, they were just beginning all this about the time I left."

"Well, Jackson ..."

A band started playing.

"What?" I could hardly hear her.

"I said ... " she raised her voice to a shout, stopped, laughed, and started again. "I said, what do you think of all this?"

The twelve-piece band blared—heavy on the brass. Neon lights flashed everywhere. On-off. On-off. Chasing. Spelling out names of establishments. Crowds of well-dressed people at the tables, crowding the bar, passing on the street outside. A din of chatter clashed with the rhythms from the bandstand.

A pert waitress set down our drinks before us on colored paper napkins. She smiled and cocked her head sideways before fluttering off.

"It's incredible," I said.

"What?" They both spoke at the same time, leaning towards me to hear better.

"It's incredible!"

Laura kept time to the music with her head. Affirmative.

"Amazing, isn't it?" said Braden.

"Huh?"

"I said, amazing what time and money can do."

We all bopped along.

"And," I said, raising my glass, "would anyone mind ... "

"Probably," said Braden.

"Good! ... if I proposed a toast?"

They raised their glasses.

"To Cassina Gambrel."

"To Cassina!"

BEFORE I LEAVE the subject of chivalry entirely, I must say one other thing. It would be a breach of the highest order, completely unpardonable, to lay bare the secrets and private lives of those who are not here to defend or speak for themselves, especially to those outside the circle. Only the dancers—if they—know the true dynamics taking place in the dance: Sexual tension, frustration, unrequited love, betrayal—the stuff of the blues. You and I, after all, are practically strangers.

Therefore, I implore you to disregard anything I have said thus far or may continue to tell you on this subject.

Yes, indeed, there is a place called Memphis, Tennessee, but her citizens are nothing like what I have portrayed them to be.

And as for Cassina, lest you should feel compelled to embark on a search for her, yourself—forget it. I made the whole thing up. Rosebud is his sled. And people—friends—true friends, that is—want only the best for each other. You believe that, don't you?

Chapter Thirteen

The Memphis Blues

THE CALL CAME early the next morning waking me from the starchy comfort of the hotel sheets.

It was Braden. "They found Cassina."

"Who ... ?"

"Meyerman."

"When ... ?"

"He called fifteen minutes ago ... "

"Jesus."

"Come ... "   "I'll be right over."

☙ ☙ ☙

"SEE BRADEN, I told you he'd come ... "

☙ ☙ ☙

THIS WENT THROUGH my head on the way to Braden's:

> "Somebody come here an' help me,
> Help me 'fore it gets too late.
> I said, come here 'n' help me,
> Help me 'fore it gets too late.

'Cause I'm finally realizin',
There's nothin' in your
ol' heart but hate."

Braden O'Brien, Laura Franklin, Cassina Gambrel, and myself sat in the saloon on Beale Street while the singer moaned on.

Everyone describes bars as "dusty" and "smoky." This one was not. Fresh paint, new wooden tables with bentwood chairs. Potted plants and ornamental metal—heavy on the brass. Someone had spent a lot of money going through archival photographs, reproducing and framing them to cover one exposed brick wall. 78's and 45's competed for space above the bar. It was all studied and carefully arranged.

"When do you think they'll be handing out cigars?" Laura asked.

Cassina surveyed the room. Twelve people other than ourselves were in the space. "Right after the darkies pass out the cotton blossoms, I reckon."

"Come on, y'all," I said, "at least they're tryin'."

"They certainly are," Braden said.

"And much too hard," said Laura.

"They's tryin' my nerves!"

Hoots and hollers from the three of them. High fives, low fives, "and here's your change."

"Come on!" I protested.

"What?" Braden asked.

"It's Beale Street." They all looked dumb. "*Beale Street*," I repeated as if emphasis would prove my point.

"Not much it ain't," said Cassina.

More laughter from Laura and Braden.

I slumped and sulked.

Cassina patted my shoulder, "Baby ... "

I shrugged her off.

Laura to the rescue: "What's it to you, Jackson?"

I looked out onto the empty sidewalks of Beale Street to a boarded up storefront across the way. A sip of whiskey swished through my mouth and was swallowed before I spoke. "It's heritage. Heritage." They were listening. "Of a place I have grown to love and will be leaving shortly. A legacy of incredible music, of spirit, of good times and struggle, and ... "

Braden cut me off, "and ... and if you don't snap out of it, *I'm* gonna' be up on that stage moanin'!"

Gentler laughter this time from Laura and Cassina.

"Piss off, Braden!" I swung around toward the small stage, adjusting my chair.

A black woman, about twenty-five years old, stood singing at a microphone backed by a piano, brass, trumpet and drums:

> "Went down to the river,
> past the Hotel Peabody."

She emphasized the first syllable of "Peabody," torturing the word to fit the song's rhythm.

"Peba-dee?" I heard Braden's voice behind me and the clink of ice in his glass.

"Shhh."

Cassina snickered.

> "Mississippi River flows
> past the Peabody."

"Well not exactly ... "

Laura laughed outright.
The singer continued:

> "I was trying to get back
> to where I used to be."

Now it was Cassina's turn, "Well, you better run fast girl."

I whipped around to face the three of them, "What is it with you people?!"

The singer finished to a smattering of applause.

Braden spoke first, "What is it with *you*?"

The manager, in black tuxedo pants, bow tie, and ruffled shirt with garters on the sleeves approached our table. "How is everything here?"

"Fine," I said quickly.

Laura spoke, "You have a nice place here."

"Thank you," the manager replied proudly. "I'm glad you like it."

Braden was silent.

I spoke. "I *do*—very much. I'm glad to see you in business."

Cassina scanned the room again. "Not much crowd tonight, though."

"No, ma'am," he said, "Reckon they're all at the Symphony."

Cassina nodded her head and smiled. " 'xpect so."

"Well," said the manager. "Is there anything I can get you?"

Without looking at the others, I replied, "We're fine, thank you."

"Well, enjoy yourselves."

"Thank you," I called after him.

Laura's head was down. Her finger made small circles in a puddle of condensation from her glass. Braden still did not speak.

Me, forever feeling compelled to fill silences, explain away everything, or to speak when given half a chance—"I'm just glad that someone's trying to keep it all alive, that's all," I said quietly.

"Keep what alive, Jackson?" Cassina put her hand on my arm.

My hand arced through the air. "This."

"This ... " Cassina mimicked my gesture. " ... this, is plastic. This ... " She gestured again. " ... is not keeping anything alive. This is not even a resurrection. This is somebody's fantasy."

Laura spoke up. "Cassina, do you remember the real Beale Street?"

"Lord, child," said Cassina. She picked up a menu from the table and fanned herself furiously. "How old do you think I am?"

Laura smiled. She rested her head on Cassina's plump shoulder and Cassina gently stroked her hair.

Seeing that I was not satisfied, Cassina said, "Jackson, some things never were. And other things," her hand took hold of mine, "run their course. Sometimes it's time for things to die."

I looked to Braden O'Brien.

"Come on, everybody up!" Cassina said. "I know what you need. I know the place we should go."

Laura was on her feet and halfway out the door.

After Braden and I settled the bill, he took my arm. "She's right, you know. She's a very wise woman."

I looked at his hand on my elbow. "That Cassina," I said, "she knows everything."

WE WALKED THEN, to the river, only a few blocks away. Along the bluffs, thousands of people sat on blankets, on folding lawn chairs, or on the grass. There was not an inch of ground to be seen that was unoccupied, so we stood, the four of us, along the top of the bluff, just over the wooden railing along Riverside Drive.

"Can y'all see? Can ya hear?" Cassina asked.

"The crowd is even bigger this year," Laura said. She looked out and down the slope upon the masses of people. "Must be over a hundred thousand!"

"I 'xpect so."

The Sunset Symphony. An annual event. Last event of the Memphis in May Festival, the Cotton Carnival, the spring ... all that. Brings a lot of things to a close. We had missed most of it. On the stage down front, a performer finished singing his rendition of "Old Man River." The crowd went wild and jumped to its feet.

Cassina leaned over and spoke to a woman standing near us. "How many is that?"

"That's his third encore!" the woman said.

Cassina clapped her hands furiously. "Reckon he'll get a fourth?"

"Prob'ly so!" The woman cheered and clapped. Laura and Braden joined in the stamping and cheering. The performer took his place as the orchestra started the song again. I looked downstream, towards the old Memphis-Arkansas Bridge. It was almost dark and the light bulbs that traced its forms reflected into the water with the deep orange color of the almost-set sun. Ripples.

The singer finished and the crowd showed its enthusiasm again. But this time he did not come out.

When the noise abated, the orchestra launched into its final number of the evening.

"Oh boy!" I heard Braden say.

Oh, those traditions, and I'm sure I'm just fantasizing, being Romantic, ascribing Symbolism and all. But who can resist "The 1812 Overture," the Mississippi River, and fireworks exploding—like chrysanthemums and comets and collisions—boom, boom, boom—now gone—fireworks in the air?

❧ ❧ ❧

I GOT TO Braden's house as fast as I possibly could without hitting anyone or anything. Fortunately, it was still before seven o'clock when I got there. This time, I bounded up the hill and the door opened. One look at Braden. One look at Laura. "What happened?"

Cassina's body had been found at last under a bridge in north Memphis, floating face down in the brown and yellow waters of the Wolf River. That infuriated me more than the fact of her death. It was not the mighty, powerful Mississippi that had claimed her, but rather a minor tributary. But there I go.

The police arrested a suspect. A scrawny, redneck sort of fellow who had taken her captive when she caught him attempting to steal the old Lincoln from the parking lot of a Midtown grocery store. Not knowing what to do with a stolen car *and* its owner, he had driven north, he told the police in a sworn statement, to an abandoned granary by the Wolf and shot her in the back as she ran, on his instructions, toward the water. That infuriated me more. He had been too stupid to even try to lie to the police.

The boy—he was twenty-two, but a boy, really—had been caught quite by accident. Realizing he now had a stolen car and that someone might begin to miss its owner, he continued north to the Missouri border and hid the car in a soybean field where he later planned to return to strip it for parts.

A week later, two children playing in a field found it and its presence was reported to the sheriff's office. By coincidence only, the thief and killer—Cassina's killer—picked the very day to begin the car's slow deconstruction that the sheriff chose to investigate. He was caught loading the car's battery into the trunk of another car he had stolen.

Further investigation revealed that there was no connection between the two—Cassina and this idiot. He had not known her. It was a random act, a chance occurrence, a "crap shot" as Cassina would say—would have said.

That was the saddest and most infuriating thing of all to me. The thing that made her death so spectacular to me was that it was so unspectacular, so *un*-dramatic, unbefitting such a one as she. I know, I know, but I don't care. Shut up and let me mourn her in my fashion, for Christ's sake. Greed, selfishness, and stupidity—sheer stupidity had killed Cassina Gambrel.

Who was she, after all, for me to weep and mourn so much? All told, there were really just a few encounters, a few blips on the screen. This enigma, why so significant, Cassina Gambrel? Cassina, Cassina, Cassina. Who was she and what had I lost? My youth, quite simply, my youth.

You see, I was Cassina and she was me and Meyerman. Braden was me and I him and Laura the both of us, too. And We became and were the city and music and fleeting, fleeting moments passing swiftly as the river. And Braden, ever the green-eyed one, wanted, like me, "everything!" and so it must have been him who arranged the Boston job offer, "too good to be true," looking guileless as a lamb all the while. But Cassina, whose role in the transaction as intermediary to Edward Meyerman (who, on analysis, had to be the true broker to a banking connection in Boston), Cassina, what of her? She wielded tremendous power. Guileless? I guess. What matter to her, really, if I stayed or went: "Sometimes it's time for things to die." And Laura, pretty Laura? Perhaps, simply, a shallow shoal.

Or maybe I'm wrong. Perhaps there was something else going on behind the scenes that I'll never know. Maybe life is not predictable and linear. Maybe it starts one way and ends another and it echoes and changes and overlaps like some strange song with recurring themes and blue notes popping up in the oddest places and that is that. Maybe the longer people are together the more they become like one another. Maybe.

But I do know some things for sure: My life in Memphis was like Memphis, itself, and Memphis is music and if you don't get that, you don't get Memphis. It's a blue note rising from a dusty yellow earth made white with cotton and it wraps itself around your honky-tonk heart and maybe, just maybe, that's why this story of Cassina Gambrel is what it is—rhythmic, and funny, and Christ, so blue.

But I know this, too: All of us were callow—more than we could ever have imagined then. Callow and dumb and sometimes petty as that boy. So if Cassina is my spirit, my youth, my friendships, my freedom, my ...

whatever, perhaps it was time for her to die. Perhaps she had died long ago. Perhaps in "growing up" we all killed her long ago. Some evil beast had devoured us.

Chapter Fourteen

*"A Cry Of Absence,
Absence In The Heart"*
—John Crowe Ransom
"Winter Remembered"

THE FUNERAL WAS a simple one, thank God, for I think that is the best way—dignity for the gathered, dignity for the deceased. The service was well attended, not packed, but a respectable number of mourners. A Sunday morning funeral. Unusual. But the minister had explained, "Every Sunday is a feast of the Resurrection." I thought that was nice.

The church was a small one, two blocks off of Chelsea Boulevard in a rundown section of North Memphis, not far from Cassina's small frame house. It was marked by a white sign in the shape of a cross that I gathered was lit from within at night. Large block letters chipped at the edge heralded, "JESUS SAVES".

Cassina had been a member of the church, a regular contributor, but not an every Sunday and Wednesday type; nevertheless, she was known by the community and its pastor, a handsome man in his thirties with a close beard and a streak of gray running through his tightly curled hair. As he stood before us in his flowing crimson robes, arms outstretched to reveal the indigo bands on the billowing sleeves, I was grateful that he was able to call her name confidently, not like so many funerals where the parishioner is obviously unknown and the minister stumbles, all but just filling in the blank space where his service book indicates, "Name of Deceased."

A nice service. Neat, tidy. I do not recall much of it. The bits I see now are all blurry, for that is how I saw them in my shock, in my grief. Unfocused snapshots in a scrapbook: The pastor leading us in prayer—the crushed, crepe flowers on the hat of a lady in front of me, head bowed. The smooth, beige walls of the room thinly covered with soot. The figurative stained-glass of the Good Shepherd holding a lamb, one pane in the lower right corner cracked so that the morning light shot through.

Then there were the flowers—wreaths and sprays of assorted sizes, ribbons stenciled "R.I.P." in gothic glitter. Yellow chrysanthemums exploding and white daisies whose petals trembled when the minister passed.

Two hymns. What is that one called that goes, "We blossom and flourish like leaves on the tree, and wither and perish but naught changeth thee"? You know the one I mean. The smell of musty hymn books and oak pews waxed to a dull gloss. The second hymn, I imagined that Cassina, in a final bit of irony had requested, but I don't know this—"Lift Every Voice and Sing."

But the thing I remember most of all is this: As the congregation rose singing to the strains of the old church organ and pall-bearers gathered by the coffin preparing to carry the remains of Cassina down the aisle one last time, I heard a voice behind me rising above the others:

> "Sing a song full of the faith
> that the dark past has taught us;
> sing a song full of the hope
> that the present has brought us."

The voice cracked a bit on the high note. I turned to see Edward Meyerman standing there, fingernails clutching the cloth binding of the worn hymnal, tears streaming down his face and onto the page.

> "Facing the rising sun,
> of our new day begun,
> let us march on,
> till victory is won."

🙞🙞🙞

    There is nothing like the silence that follows a funeral. It is a thick, heavy thing, interrupted occasionally by the clatter of cups and dishes, the murmur of voices, "Can I get you something?" "Do you care for more?" The scratching sound a worn tissue makes rubbing the raw space beneath a red nose. A bell ringing somewhere in the distance: "Remember ... Remember ...."
    "No, no thank you. I'm fine really."
    Braden at the door, the last guests leaving—"Thank you so much." "We'll see you next week." Door latching shut.

Chapter Fifteen

"The Movin' Finger Done Writ"
—Cassina Gambrel

"WELL, THAT'S IT. The moving finger, as Cassina would say, has done writ."

I left the next day. No calls. No goodbyes. Jelly where my spine should be.

The trip had been brief—Thursday, Friday, Saturday, Sunday. Shorter than I planned. Quicker than I expected. Quick. Not quick enough. Not long enough. Too long. Long enough to know something. Something.

Shortest possible route to the airport. No farewell tour. No spin through the old neighborhood—the college, the house, the sights. Clean break. A fast getaway.

If my initial hours in Memphis had taken on a dreamlike quality, the time back in Boston was something a step beyond. Different even from the feeling at the funeral. Numb. Gauzy. Hmm. What's the word? Only if you've been in that space will you know. I got off the "T," thought of taking a cab. Decided to walk. *Good for me: Air. Exercise.* Began to climb the hill toward the old monument. Out of breath. Getting old. *Ha! No, you ain't, Jackson.*

Key in the lock. Familiar space. Books, papers. The same old thing. Cat out of hiding—rubbing my legs, getting between my feet when I walk. Damn thing. Stupid thing. Fucking, god-damned, stupid thing.

Calls to Ben. Update him. I'll start the day-classes again Wednesday. Let Tuesday night go. Call students later. Activate the old phone-tree. Damage control. The trip didn't take nearly so long. Ready to go a.s.a.p.

"Shuah?" Ben asked on the telephone.

"Yes."

Thank Ben again. Covering my butt. Same ol' same ol'.

Early to bed, right after the news. No sleep—well, maybe a little. Roll and toss. Dream of water. Up at two to vomit. *Damn airline food.* Must be that. Jet lag? Hmm. Tired? Yes. No.

Next day, the routine. Get on track. *Come on boy, you can do it.* No, I can't. Yes, yes, yes. Up on that old horse. Up we go! Upsy-daisy! Ugh. Pick up the mail. Pick up the papers. Tip the kid. Nothing new. Doorbell rings. *Shit, what now?*

Overnight courier. Package foah you, suh. Thank you. What could that be? Too big for a breadbox—Yuk, yuk. Flat, large. Three feet by four. Thanks very much.

Open the box. Rip off the paper. A note. Who is this from?

"Dear Jackson, I forgot to give you this.
My senior project from our college days.
Love ... "

A picture. And a damn fine one, too. "Well, I'll be, what about it, and bless your heart, Braden ... " Four figures on a boat—one of those touristy things, an old paddle-wheeler. Four people. Arms around each other. Backs to the viewer, their heads looking up. Fireworks. Fireworks in a Southern sky.

How long had it been since I had done such a thing? Cry, I mean. Blubber like a little baby. Pardon me, but would the band be so kind....

NOT MUCH TO say anymore, I guess. "The movin' finger ... ", you know, and all that. Reality sets in. Sets in fast. Nothing to do. Practicality—a contract. A term to finish. A year more to go. Another year to make a change ... and to look for Cassina Gambrel.

Author's Note

Cassina Gambrel Was Missing is a work of fiction. While I have drawn on my personal knowledge of Memphis, Tennessee and surrounding areas, many geographical references may be altered for the purpose of enhancing the narrative. At other times, I have endeavored to be as true as possible to my recollections of that city and of the historical events which transpired during the time span of the book. The reason for that is obvious: I wanted to make as realistic a story as possible and set out to accomplish that task by placing the characters in as much of an accurate and detailed setting as possible. Jackson claims that he and his friends were "very much changed and changing" at that time of their lives. So was the city of Memphis. The changes in the setting and the characters are reflective of each other and, I hope, the reader will see that at times the characters and the setting are metaphors for each other just as Cassina, despite all of Braden's protestations (and there is truth in them), is a metaphor for something larger.

While any resemblance to any actual persons, living or dead, is purely coincidental, I relied heavily on contemporary news accounts of the municipal workers' strikes of 1978—a real event—in Chapter Three, *I'll Take My Stand*, and wish to acknowledge three sources particularly: *US News and World Report*, August 28, 1978; D.A. Williams and others writing for *Newsweek*, August 28, 1978; and Michael Daly writing for *New Times*, October 2, 1978.

One further note: The Yiddish word *shvarzer* used by Cassina in Chapter One is a derogatory term for "Negro" whose dynamic equivalent in English can be inferred by the reader. Certainly the word is offensive. Jackson knows this—hence his reaction to hearing Cassina say it. Cassina, who "knows everything," knows that too. Her intent in telling Jackson the story is to relate the skillful and subtle way she turned the tables on Esther Meyerman and to test Jackson. By now the reader realizes that Cassina Gambrel is nobody's fool. Use of the word in this work is clearly not meant to offend, nor is it meant to condone racism (in fact, quite the opposite), but to reveal character and an unfortunate fact of the world that the characters inhabit and struggle against.

About the Author

William Watkins is a freelance writer and producer whose television work has appeared nationally on the CBS News broadcast *Up to the Minute*. He has also worked in media relations at the CBS Television Network in both its News and Entertainment divisions as well as at SW Networks (Sony) in New York for the kickoff of *The Mario Cuomo Show* on radio.

Prior to that, Watkins worked in the religion and human rights fields as a chaplain for AIDS patients and in various capacities at the national headquarters of Amnesty International, USA in New York. He received his Master of Divinity degree from the General Theological Seminary and also studied at New York Theological Seminary.

Bill is a native of Greenville, South Carolina and lived for several years in Memphis, Tennessee where he received a Bachelor of Arts Degree in Communication Arts from Southwestern at Memphis (now Rhodes College).

He lives in New York City where he is currently working on his second novel and a television documentary.